1,000,000 Books

are available to read at

Forgotten Books

www.ForgottenBooks.com

Read online
Download PDF
Purchase in print

ISBN 978-1-331-48068-6
PIBN 10195981

This book is a reproduction of an important historical work. Forgotten Books uses state-of-the-art technology to digitally reconstruct the work, preserving the original format whilst repairing imperfections present in the aged copy. In rare cases, an imperfection in the original, such as a blemish or missing page, may be replicated in our edition. We do, however, repair the vast majority of imperfections successfully; any imperfections that remain are intentionally left to preserve the state of such historical works.

Forgotten Books is a registered trademark of FB &c Ltd.
Copyright © 2018 FB &c Ltd.
FB &c Ltd, Dalton House, 60 Windsor Avenue, London, SW19 2RR.
Company number 08720141. Registered in England and Wales.

For support please visit www.forgottenbooks.com

1 MONTH OF FREE READING

at

www.ForgottenBooks.com

By purchasing this book you are eligible for one month membership to ForgottenBooks.com, giving you unlimited access to our entire collection of over 1,000,000 titles via our web site and mobile apps.

To claim your free month visit: www.forgottenbooks.com/free195981

* Offer is valid for 45 days from date of purchase. Terms and conditions apply.

English
Français
Deutsche
Italiano
Español
Português

www.forgottenbooks.com

Mythology Photography **Fiction** Fishing Christianity **Art** Cooking Essays Buddhism Freemasonry Medicine **Biology** Music **Ancient Egypt** Evolution Carpentry Physics Dance Geology **Mathematics** Fitness Shakespeare **Folklore** Yoga Marketing **Confidence** Immortality Biographies Poetry **Psychology** Witchcraft Electronics Chemistry History **Law** Accounting **Philosophy** Anthropology Alchemy Drama Quantum Mechanics Atheism Sexual Health **Ancient History Entrepreneurship** Languages Sport Paleontology Needlework Islam **Metaphysics** Investment Archaeology Parenting Statistics Criminology **Motivational**

THE FLYING BO'SUN
A MYSTERY OF THE SEA

BY
ARTHUR MASON

NEW YORK
HENRY HOLT AND COMPANY

COPYRIGHT, 1920
BY
HENRY HOLT AND COMPANY

PS
3525
M38f

DEDICATED
TO THE MEMORY OF
MY MOTHER
WHOSE SYMPATHY MADE
IT POSSIBLE FOR ME
TO GO TO SEA

CONTENTS

CHAPTER I
Off for the South Seas, with Few Clothes but a Stout Heart 3

CHAPTER II
The Storm — Tattered and Torn but Still on the Ocean 13

CHAPTER III
Beecham's Pills Are Worth a Guinea Though They Cost but Eighteen Pence 25

CHAPTER IV
Personalities — Omens and Superstitions of Old Charlie 33

CHAPTER V
The Shark — "To Hell with Shark and Ship" 44

CHAPTER VI
The Tin-Plate Fight — One-Eyed Riley Triumphs 52

CONTENTS

CHAPTER VII
IN WHICH THE CAPTAIN WOUNDS HIS HAND . . 61

CHAPTER VIII
THE BO'SUN LIGHTS — THE CAPTAIN'S DEATH . 68

CHAPTER IX
THE SHOWDOWN — SWANSON TAKES THE COUNT . 76

CHAPTER X
BURIAL AT SEA — IN WHICH RILEY OFFICIATES . 83

CHAPTER XI
ASTRAL INFLUENCES — THE CREW'S VERSION OF THE UNKNOWN 91

CHAPTER XII
THE COOK'S WATCH — MATERIALISM VERSUS ASTRALISM 100

CHAPTER XIII
HIGHER INTELLIGENCE — A VISIT FROM OUT THE SHADOWS 107

CHAPTER XIV
CHRISTMAS DAY — OUR UNWILLING GUEST THE DOLPHIN 117

CONTENTS

CHAPTER XV
CRIMP AND SAILOR — THE COOK'S MARXIAN EFFORT 123

CHAPTER XVI
THE MONTANA COWBOY — A HORSE-MARINE ADVENTURE 130

CHAPTER XVII
THE FRAGRANT SMELL OF THE ALLURING PALMS . 141

CHAPTER XVIII
SUVA HARBOR — THE REEF AND THE LIGHTHOUSES 146

CHAPTER XIX
INTRODUCING CAPTAIN KANE, MRS. FAGAN AND MRS. FAGAN'S BAR 151

CHAPTER XX
REMINISCENCES OF OLD CLIPPER DAYS 158

CHAPTER XXI
UNLOADING CARGO — AGAIN THE MASTER — NATIVE POLICE 163

CHAPTER XXII
SHORE LEAVE — THE WEB-TOED SAILOR — THE MISSIONARY SHIP 173

CONTENTS

CHAPTER XXIII
Fiji Royalty — Local Color — Visitors to the Ship 187

CHAPTER XXIV
A Drive with Captain Kane — Razorback Rampant 194

CHAPTER XXV
Homeward Bound — The Stowaway . . . 202

CHAPTER XXVI
The Mysterious Hindoo 211

CHAPTER XXVII
The Hurricane 220

CHAPTER XXVIII
The Master Returns 228

CHAPTER XXIX
The Home Port 238

INTRODUCTORY NOTE

Hardship is a stern master, from whom we part willingly.

But it is often true that real men learn thereby to handle their fellow-men, to love them, and to make the most of their own manhood. In no class is this more marked than among those who have been formed by the training of the sea.

Hundreds have lost their lives there, hundreds more have been coarsened through ignorance and because of rough living, but the survivors, who have used what God gave them of brain and muscle to the best advantage, are a lot of men to be trusted mightily.

I am proud to have known such men, and to have lived the life that made them what they are, and, above all, proud to have sailed before the time when steam began to drive the square-rigger from the seas.

Therefore I have ventured to set before the

INTRODUCTORY NOTE

public a narrative of my own experience, somewhat condensed, but little changed, even in some parts that may seem hard to believe, but sailors are known to be superstitious. Should this book fall into the hands of other sailors, I think it will interest them, and landsmen may care for the truthful record of a day that is almost gone.

A. M.

THE FLYING BO'SUN

CHAPTER I

Off for the South Seas, With Few Clothes but a Stout Heart

Her name was the "Wampa," graceful to look at, with her tall and stately masts, rigged with fore and aft sails. She was known as one of the fastest schooners sailing to the Southern Seas.

That afternoon in December found her loading lumber in a rather quaint saw-mill town on the Puget Sound. Her Captain, who was a Swede, was tall and handsome and had none of the earmarks of the old salt. He seemed to be very nervous as he walked up and down the poop deck. Once he called out, "Olsen, put one more truck load on, then get your deck lashings ready. She is down now, she has eight inches of water on the after deck." With that he jumped ashore saying, "If I can find a mate we will sail this evening."

As I stood there viewing her yacht-like lines and noticing the shark's fin on her bowsprit,

I was satisfied that she was in a class by herself.

As he turned to go I said, "Captain, do you need a mate?"

"Are you a mate? If you can get your trunk and bag on board we will sail within an hour."

"But I have neither bag nor trunk. If you want me you will have to take me as I stand."

"Have you a sextant?"

"No, but I can borrow one from the tug boat captain. He never leaves sight of land. I am sure he will rent it to me for this voyage."

"Very well," said he. "Get your sextant, and we will find some way of getting rubber boots and oil skins," and off he strolled up to the Company's office.

Two hours later, with the deck lashings set up, tug boat alongside, everything ready for our voyage, our Captain sang out "Let go forward, starboard your helm, Murphy,"— the tug boat gave a "toot, toot," and we were off for the open sea.

By this time I had a chance to size up the crew. The second mate was a short, thick, heavy-set Dane, seemingly a good sailor. Our cook was a greasy, dirty-looking German and, from what few words I had with him, showed that he was a Socialist. The sailors were Dagoes, Irish, Swedes and Russian Finns.

With the wind freshening as we neared the open sea, the Captain sang out, "Mr. Mate, loose and set the foresail and main jib." With the gaskets off I gave the order to hoist away. I noticed one very large Swede hardly pulling a pound. I say "large"; he stood six feet or more and weighed upwards of two hundred. "What is your name?" said I.

He looked me over and said, "Why?"

I said "You must pull some more or you will never know what your name was."

I decided that now was the time to take care of this sea lawyer. The foresail was about half up. I gave the order to make fast.

I said to this big Swede, "Come here, I have something to say to you."

"If you want me come and get me."

"Very good," and with that I caught him with a strangle hold and dragged him across the deck. Then I released him. "Now tell me what your name is."

He looked amazed and humiliated, and in a hoarse voice said, "Swanson."

I said, "Swanson, I want you to work, and work your share."

He said, "You ban good steerman."

Steerman is the Swedish for mate.

"Well then, Swanson, let us get those sails up."

Just then the Captain came forward saying, "What in Hell is the matter? Why don't you get those sails on her?"

"Captain," I replied, pointing to Swanson, "this man did not quite understand me. Hoist away on your throat and peak halyards."

Up went the foresail as if by magic, then the main jib and inner jib, the tug boat gave three long whistles, signalling "let go your hawser."

I heard the Captain sing out, "Mr. Mate, up with your mainsail and spanker."

"Aye, aye, sir."

In a few minutes all sail was set.

The Captain gave the course south one-half west and went down below. I immediately took my departure, and entered it in the log book. The wind was free, about two points abaft the beam. I put the taff-rail log over the side and settled down for our trip to the sunny south. As it was getting late in the evening, I went forward to talk to the second mate about picking our watches.

It is always customary for the mate to take the ship out, and the captain to bring her home. This meant that I would have eight hours watch the first night out. The mate has always the privilege of choosing the first man, and by doing this the big Swede fell to the second mate. Because I was sure I would have trouble with him, I tossed him into the starboard watch. After the watches were set, and the wheel relieved, I heard the supper bell ring.

As I was hungry I made for the cabin, and took a seat across from the Captain. Out of the pantry came the Socialist cook with two plates of soup.

The Captain was not very talkative, thinking I was a low-grade mate, since I was minus trunk and bag. The cook eyed me rather curiously when I passed up the onion soup. I understood later that it was only on rare occasions he ever gave way to cooking so delicate a dish. Should any one be so misguided as to refuse to eat it they might count the galley their enemy forever. With supper over I went on deck to relieve the second mate. He looked to me as if there would be no trouble between him and the cook and onion soup. As it was now my watch from eight to twelve, I had the side lights lit and my watch came on deck to relieve the wheel and look-out.

I may mention here some of the sailors in my watch. Well, Broken-Nose Pete took his turn at the wheel, and One-Eyed Riley took the look-out. Then there was Dago Joe and a Dane by the name of Nelson, who seemed rather quiet and unassuming. Also Charlie who was forever looking up at the clouds.

The wind was freshening up and she was listing over with the lee rail in the water. I went aft to take a look at the log. She was doing ten knots and doing it easy. "Well," thought I, "if she can do ten with lower sails and topsails, she will do twelve with the fisherman's staysails on." So I gave the order to bend and hoist away and no sooner were they set and sheets flattened aft than she began to feel them.

It seemed that those staysails were all that were holding her back to show me she was worthy of the shark's fin on the flying jib boom. The Captain was walking up and down the poop deck smoking a cigar, seemingly in good humor with his new mate. As I was going aft, I noticed that she had broached to somewhat. She seemed to want to shake herself clear of all her canvas. I ran to the man at the wheel: "What in Hell is the matter with you? Can't you steer?" I cried.

"Yes, sir, I can steer very well, but since you put those staysails on her I can hardly hold her in the water."

"Keep her on her course," I warned him, "or you will hear from me." I went to the rail to look at the log. It was getting dark, and I had to strike a match to see. Sure enough, she was making twelve and a quarter.

Just then the Captain came up and told me to take in the staysails, as she was laboring too much. I was going to protest, but, on second thoughts, I bowed to the ways of deep-water captains: "Obey orders, if you break owners."

"Captain, you have a pretty smart little ship here."

"Yes," said he. "She passed everything on her last trip to Mayhew, New Caledonia, but one has got to know and understand her to get the best out of her."

Right here I knew he was giving me a dig for daring to set the staysails without his orders.

Tossing the butt of his cigar overboard, he started to go below saying "Call me if the wind freshens up or changes. But call me at eight bells anyway."

The night grew brighter. A half moon was trying to fight her way out from behind a cloud, ever-hopeful of throwing her silver rays on the good ship "Wampa." With the sound of the wash on the prow, and the easy balanced roll, with occasional spray from windward, I felt that after all the sea was the place for me.

Just then the lookout shouted, "Light on the starboard bow, sir."

I said, "All right," and reached for the binoculars. A full rigged ship was approaching on the port tack.

"Port your helm, let her come to." When we had her on the lee, I sang out, "Steady as she goes."

As we passed under her quarter, what a beautiful living thing she seemed in the shadows of the night,— and in my dreaming I was near forgetting to keep our ship on her course again. By this time hunger, that familiar genius of those who walk the decks, was upon me again. Nothing tastes better than the time-honored lunch late during the watches at night. I found for myself some cold meat, bread and butter, and coffee in the pantry.

I called the second mate as it was nearing eight bells, twelve o'clock. I felt tired and sleepy and knew that nothing short of a hurricane would awake me from twelve to four.

Up on deck Dago Joe struck eight bells, I took the distance run on the log, and was turning around to go down and call the Captain, when Swanson came aft to relieve the wheel. He looked me over very critically and muttered something to himself. As I went down the companion way to report to the Old Man, I saw the Socialist cook standing in my room.

"Here, Mr. Mate, is a blanket for you. I know you have no bedding."

I thanked him and thought, "Well, the Socialist cook is kind and observant and Socialism is not bad after all."

I called the Captain, then went to my room for a well-earned sleep.

CHAPTER II

The Storm: Tattered and Torn But Still On the Ocean

Olsen, the second mate, called me at four o'clock. When I came on deck the sky was overcast, and looked like rain. From the log I found that she had made thirty-eight miles during the middle watch.

"If she keeps this up for forty-eight hours," I thought, "we shall be abreast of San Francisco." She could not travel fast enough for me, going South, for with only one suit of clothes and a Socialist blanket, latitude 46° north in December was no place for me.

The cook came aft with a mug of coffee that had the kick of an army mule. It is seldom the cook on a wind-jammer ever washes the coffee pot. Pity the sailor, forward or aft, who would criticize the cooking! One must always flatter the pea-soup, and the salt-horse, and particularly the bread-pudding, if one expects any consideration.

The Captain stuck his head out of the companion-way, and from his expression I knew that he was minus the mocha. "How is the wind?" said he.

"It has hauled a little aft, sir, about northwest."

"Get the staysails on and steer south," and he dived below, looking for the cook, I suppose.

I went forward to see if any sails needed sweating up. I called Broken-Nosed Pete and Riley to take a pull on the main boom topinlift.

"Pete, what happened to your nose?"

"It is a long yarn," said he, "and some night in the tropics I shall spin it."

It was now breaking day. The cook was coming forward to the galley, singing "Shall we always work for wages?" Behind him strolled Toby, the big black cat, who seemed very much in command of the ship. Seven bells, and breakfast, some of the same beefsteak, with the elasticity of a sling-shot, and other trimmings.

The Captain seemed more talkative. "I understand that we are bound for Suva, Fiji Islands," said I.

"Yes, and I expect to make it in about fifty

days, for with this breeze and a smooth sea, we shall be with the flying-fish before long."

"That will be very convenient for me, Sir." ("No, no more coffee, thank you, Steward.")

("Steward" is more appropriate than "Cook," and gives him a dignity befitting his position in the presence of officers, while forward he is pleased to be called "Doctor." But that title is seldom used, as it depends upon the good-nature of the crew.)

"Warm sailing will indeed be convenient for you," said the Captain. "How did you lose your clothes? Shipwrecked? Here, Steward, take away this Bourbon brand," (handing him the condensed milk). "I see the flies have found it."

"No, sir, not shipwrecked. My last trip, from Guaymas, was full of incidents, especially in the Gulf of California. It took us six days, with light, baffling winds and thunder-storms, to make Cape St. Lucas. While we were rounding the Cape, lightning struck the mizzen-top, destroying the mutton-leg spanker and setting fire to the chafing gear. Luckily for us, the sails were damp. As it was the lightning ran forward on the tryatic stay, and broke our forestay at the night-head."—

"Steward," interrupted the Captain anxiously, "don't feed Toby too much. That old lime-juicer that was lying next to us at the loading dock was alive with rats, and I am afraid that we have our share. You say," turning to me, "that the forestay was carried away?"

"Yes, sir, and that was not all. When she pitched aft, the spring-stays buckled, and snapped our topmast clean out of her. We let all the halyards go by the run. I have been going to sea for many years, but never have I seen a mess like the old 'Roanoke.' With the topmast hanging in the cross-trees, sails, booms and gaffs swinging all over the deck, she looked as if she had been through a hurricane. But after cutting away the topmast rigging, and letting the topmast go by the run (watching the roll, of course, so that they would be sure to clear the bulwark rail), we got a ten-inch hawser from the lazarette to replace the one that had been carried away. With the deck cleared, and lower sails set, she was able to lay her course

THE STORM 17

again, and after thirty-two days we crippled into port.

"While lying in Bellingham, our port of discharge, I was relating my experience to a few old salts, men with whom I had sailed in other seas. There happened to be a land-lubber who questioned my story. He called me a liar. I said, 'You beat it.' He reached for his hip pocket. Instantly I swung for his jaw. He went down and I walked away. Later I met the night policeman. 'You had better get across the line till this blows over,' he said. 'The doctor says that he has a broken jaw.'

"In Vancouver shipping was light, so I took a job in a logging-camp running an old ship's donkey-engine hauling logs. Wells, the logging company went broke, and I with them, and that is my reason for not having any clothes."

"What became of the man with the broken jaw?" asked the Captain.

"I heard that he bought a gas motor cycle; they were new in the East then. He had one shipped to Bellingham, and ran it without a muffler. It made such a noise that horses ran away, and chickens flew about, and eventually the townspeople ran him out of town."

It was now past eight bells, and from the angry sound of Olsen's feet on the deck above, I knew that he could take care of what steak was left.

"Well," said the Captain, "that reminds me of an experience I once had on the 'Glory of the Seas,' off River Plate. Not an electrical storm, but worse, a squall without warning. You have to relieve Olsen now, so I will finish some other time in your watch below."

The cook was in the pantry, humming his favorite song, omitting the words.

It was my watch below, but I remained long enough on deck for Olsen to finish his breakfast. Away towards the eastward the sky was blood red, and the northwest wind was dying out. If the old sailor's adage holds good, then "A red sky in the morning, sailors take warning." I had been familiar with those signs in the Northern Pacific for years. In the winter time it usually meant a gale. When Olsen returned, I laid out the work to be done during the forenoon. "Get together your reef-earrings, have your halyards coiled down ready for running," I

THE STORM

said. "We may have a blow before long."

"Yaw," said the Dane, "I don't like the sky to the eastward."

In the cabin, the Captain was sorting over some old letters. "Here," said he, "is a picture of my two boys. They are living in Berkeley. Their mother died two years ago while I was in South America. The doctor said it was T. B." With tears in his eyes he said, "I suppose it had to be, but don't you know, they are quite happy. They are living with their aunt. Oh, children forget so soon, so soon." Picking up the pictures, and with a look of hatred in his eyes he said, "The sea is no place for a married man."

At seven bells I came on deck to take the meridian altitude of the sun. It was now partly cloudy, and hard to get a clear horizon, as the sun would dive in and out from behind the clouds. What little wind there was came from the southeast.

"I guess we shall have to rely on your dead reckoning," said the Captain, "the barometer is dropping, and it looks as if we are in for a gale."

At four o'clock in the afternoon it commenced

to blow from the southeast. We took in staysails, topsails and flying-jib. She was close-hauled and headed southwest. In the first dog-watch the wind increased.

"Call all hands," said the Captain, "we must reef her down."

The spanker-boom projected over the stern about twenty feet. It was no easy matter reefing this sail, with the wind and sea increasing and her shipping an occasional sea. There was some danger of one's being washed overboard and very little chance of saving a life. But now was the time to find out if our sailors were from the old school. I loved the storms, and the wild raging seas and angry skies,— no sea gull ever enjoyed the tempest more than I.

"Here you, Johnson, Nelson and Swanson, lay out on the boom, haul out and pass your reef-earring, and be quick about it."

Swanson said: "I'll not go out there. The foot-rope is too short."

"By God, you'll go out there if I have to haul you with a handy billy."

"Yes, damn you, get out there," roared the Captain. "You call yourself a sailor; it is a beachcomber you are!" The Captain worked himself into a rage. "By Heavens, we will make sailors of you before this trip is over."

Swanson with a look of rage, decided that an alternative of the boom-end with an occasional dip into the raging sea underneath and elevation on high as she rolled, was much preferable to what he could expect should he refuse to obey orders. With the spanker and mainsail close-reefed we were pretty snug.

"If the wind increases it will be necessary to heave her to; that will do; the watch below," said I.

Old Charlie was coiling down ropes. "Mr. Mate, look out for Swanson, I just heard him say that this ship is too small for you and him. He is very disagreeable in the foc'sle. He and One-Eyed Riley came near having a scrap over the sour beans at noon to-day."

Three hours later the wind increased to a living gale. Before we could let go the halyards it blew our foresail away.

. "My God," cried the Captain, "and brand new. Just begged my owners for it. Six hundred dollars gone to Hell! Get the mainsail and inner jib off lively. Heave her to under the main jib." Speaking to the man at the wheel: "Don't let her go off, damn you, let her come to, and put your wheel in 'midships."

Throughout the night the wind kept up, with the seas battering our deckload, until there was danger of having it washed overboard. But about seven o'clock in the morning it abated some. The old ship had the expression of a wet water-spaniel coming out of the water before shaking himself. Defiant as she was to race away from storm and strife, she was hopelessly crippled by the mountainous sea that was trying to swallow her up in its angry roll.

"Never mind about anything," said the Captain, "get the damned old spare foresail up anyway, we will have to patch it and get it onto her. Olsen, how do the stores and flour look? Yes, it is aft on the port side."

"The rats have torn two sacks of flour open, sir."

"Great God, have they gotten in there already? Run and get Toby, and put him down there, I will attend to the lazarette hatch myself from now on."

THE STORM

So saying, he walked to the rail and levelled his glass at an approaching ship.

Out of the murky horizon loomed up the U. S. transport "Dix," with troops bound for Manila to aid in the capture of Aguinaldo. As she passed us to windward Old Charlie remarked, "There will be few aboard of her to eat breakfast this morning, the way she pitches and rolls."

It was plain to be seen that the Captain was in no mood for comedy this particular morning. With the loss of his new foresail, and rats in the flour, and worst of all forgetting to wind the chronometer, a fatal result of his preoccupation with the storm, he was the picture of a man doomed to despair, and I, for one, approached him very gingerly.

With a look of disdain at Old Charlie, he said, "To Hell with breakfast! All you beachcombers think of is eating. Haul the gaff to windward. Bend on the old foresail, or we shall be blown clear across to Japan."

Towards noon the wind let up a little, enough to carry lower sails. Even with a heavy sea we were able to make five and one-half knots, but were off our course four points, as the wind was still south southeast.

"Mr. Mate, the Captain wants to see you."

"All right, Olsen."

In the cabin the Captain was walking in a circle. "Damn it all," he cried, "why couldn't *you* remind me to wind the chronometer?"

"I did not know that you had one on board, sir."

"Hell and damnation! Go to sea without a chronometer? Who ever heard of such a thing!" Swinging his arms wildly over his head, he said, "Where in blazes did you go to sea?"

"Captain," said I, "I have made a twenty-thousand mile trip without a chronometer with old Captain Sigelhorst in the bark "Quickstep," not so long ago. We can surely get our position from a passing ship, and if not, we can make land, say off San Diego, and easily correct our position for Greenwich time."

"Well, it is a damned poor business, anyway."

Just then we were interrupted by Olsen, who reported to the Captain that Swanson was sick and refused to come on deck.

CHAPTER III

BEECHAM'S PILLS ARE WORTH A GUINEA THOUGH THEY COST BUT EIGHTEEN PENCE

In those days, twenty years ago, sailing schooners had few men before the mast, and every man was called upon to do a man's work. If one of the crew were sick, it usually caused a great deal of trouble both fore and aft. In bad and stormy weather it was not uncommon for the old and seasoned sailor to play sick, provided he could get away with it. The usual symptom was lame back, so that the appetite might not be questioned. When the ship would emerge into fine weather, marvel of marvels, the sailor would recover in a moment.

"Sick, is he?" said the Captain, and pointed to me, saying: "Go forward and see what the trouble is."

"I am sure," I replied, "that he will be on deck before long, sir."

"All I have in the medicine chest is pills, yes, damn it, pills," and he waved me forward.

In the forecastle Swanson was lying in his bunk with the blankets pulled up over his head, sound asleep, and beside him, lying on a bench, was all that remained of a breakfast piece of hardtack, and a large bone, with teethmarks in the gristle.

"Well," thought I, "if he is getting as close to the bone as this, he can't be very sick." I awoke him, saying: "What is the matter with you, Swanson? Why aren't you on deck? This is not your watch below."

He rolled over as if in great agony.

"Mr. Mate, I ban very sick man."

"Where are you sick?"

"I ban sick on this side," pointing to the right side.

"Stick out your tongue. Yes, indeed, you are a very sick man. Can't eat, I suppose." He answered me with a grunt as if in mortal pain.

I went aft and asked the Captain for a few pills. "Give me five."

"Hell, take ten. How is he?"

"I will have him on deck in a few hours, sir."

After Swanson had swallowed the last pill I

said, "You are feeling much easier now, aren't you? Of course, this treatment will relieve you, but only temporarily. I am positive that you have a very bad case of appendicitis."

This seemed to please the Swede very much. "But," said I, "it is very unfortunate that we are running into another storm, the pitching and rolling of the ship will be bad for you."

He looked me fair in the eye, saying, "Why?"

"Well, it may be either death or an operation for you very soon."

"I tank de pain go down," pointing to his hip.

"Yes, Swanson, that is the most pronounced symptom of all," I said, pathetically. "You lie still while I go aft and see what kind of cutlery the Captain has."

"Captain," I asked, when I was once more on deck, "what kind of pills were those that you just gave me for Swanson?"

"Beecham's pills, and five is a very large dose. I have had them by me for years. As a boy I was introduced to them by the North Sea fishermen," he proceeded solemnly. "You know they advertise them on the sails of luggers, smacks and sloops, in fact, wherever you look in the North Sea, Irish Sea or English Channel you can always see Beecham's Pills go sailing by."

Towards evening the weather broke clear with the wind hauling towards the northeast and eastward, and the prospects looked good for better weather. About nine o'clock the cook came running aft, crying, "Mr. Mate, Swanson is very sick, and the crew think that he is going to die."

"What is the matter with him now?" said I, very coolly.

"He has terrible cramps. Russian-Finn John and Broken-Nosed Pete have all they can do to hold him in the bunk."

"You go to the galley, steward, and get a quart of warm water. You can give it to him while John and Pete hold him, and I have no doubt that in this case Riley will be glad to help. Is that he groaning?"

"Yes," said the Steward, trembling, "he is in terrible agony."

"Have you given him anything to eat for supper?"

"My God, yes, he has gorged himself on corned beef and cabbage."

"Well," thought I, "he has reason to roll and groan."

"Get that hot water," I continued aloud, "and be quick about it. If anything happens to him after this you will be to blame. The idea of feeding corned beef and cabbage to a man with a high fever!" The cook waited to hear no more. All I could see was the dirty apron flying for the galley.

The Captain, hearing us talking from the cabin, shouted out, "What is all that noise up there?"

"Nothing much, sir; she is now laying her course with the wind free." This was hoping to distract him with weather conditions from asking whom I dared to talk with on the poop deck. Discipline must be adhered to on windjammers. Mates and second mates give their orders in whispers, but never loud enough to awaken His Majesty the Captain. The mates are held in high esteem by the crew when they see the Captain conversing with them, but for one of the crew to come and carry on a conversation with an officer when he is aft in his sacred precinct, the poop deck, is considered a crime, and ranks almost next to mutiny. Evidently he thought that I was giving some orders to the crew, for he closed the porthole, and did not ask me the question.

On my way forward to see how the steward was getting along with his mission, and while abreast the forerigging, Old Charlie tapped me on the shoulder and pointed toward the forecastle saying: " Mr. Mate, Swanson is a very sick man. He thinks that you have given him poison, sir, and "— stepping close to me, " I feel that something is going to happen on this ship."

"What makes you think that?" said I.

Pulling his old hairy cap down around his ears, and settling down for a long yarn, he said: " In the winter of 1875 I was in a ship off the Cape of Good Hope. We lost three sailors overboard —".

"I am in a hurry, Charlie, you will be too long —"

"I have had queer dreams lately, sir," he interrupted.

"Tell me some other time," said I, "I must see the Swede."

Down in the forecastle Riley was comforting

Swanson in the uncertain language of the sea, while the cook held his head, eyeing me, and saying very softly, "I don't think that it is the cabbage, sir."

"What is it then," said I, "I only gave two grains of quinine to reduce his fever. Stand back, there, so that I can get a look at him. How are you now, Swanson?" As I said this, the words of the advertisement occurred to me, "Beecham's Pills are worth a guinea, though they cost but eighteen pence."

There was no bluffing with the Swede. He was sick in good earnest now. "I think I ban poisoned, Mr. Mate."

"No, Swanson, you have not been poisoned. You must be operated on, and at once."

"Begob, sir," said Riley, with a wink at me, "and sure it is myself that knows how to carve. I will be after helping you, sir."

"Thank you, Riley, it is a dirty job, and I should much prefer that you would do it."

"Let me up," yelled the Swede.

"Hold him down, men," said I. "You know that he is out of his head from fever, and it would be dangerous for him to get up until after the operation." It now dawned upon Swanson that I was in earnest about the operation. For a one-eyed Irishman and his enemy to cut a hole in him was more than he could bear. With a wild plunge that hurled his captors to right and left, he jumped from his bunk, and raced for his life up the ladder that led to the deck.

Seven bells in the morning, and with a fine sailing breeze, we were leaving behind the sleet and storms for those who sail the northern latitudes.

"I saw Swanson on deck this morning," said the Captain.

"Yes, sir, he is better. I don't think that we shall have any more trouble from him in that direction."

CHAPTER IV

OMENS AND SUPERSTITIONS OF OLD CHARLIE

Four days later a tramp steamer hove in sight. We signaled him, and asked for his position. He signaled back, giving latitude and longitude. He was about a mile to the eastward of us. We set and wound our chronometer, and considered this luck indeed, as the Captain expressed it. He seemed quite happy, and, with an expression of confidence on his face, remarked:

"Well, we are all right again. You know I was very much worried about forgetting to wind the chronometer. I have been master for fourteen years, and this is the first time that I have neglected to do it. I have heard from old-timers that it is considered a bad omen."

"I don't believe in any such superstitions," said I.

Here he called to the cook, who was throwing slop overboard from the galley: "Have you given Toby any water today?"

"Yessir," said the cook, and cursed a large black and white gull for eating more than his share of the scraps that were floating by. "Toby wants for nothing, sir. In fact, he has been getting out of the lazarette lately."

The Captain did not hear this last remark. He was watching the remains from the galley to see if there was any waste. Old sailors say they can tell how ships feed by the number of gulls who follow in her wake.

(Now follow some extracts from my diary, kept during a portion of this trip.)

For the last week we have been having fine weather. The cook and crew seem to be very friendly. I notice that during the dog-watch from six to eight they gather around the mainmast. There the cook has a barrel in which he freshens salt meat. In this watch he puts it to soak. This evening he must have been carried away with his subject, for he was talking loudly and very excitedly, exclaiming:

"That is it exactly, and here we are. What are we getting? Nothing. And to think that we are the slaves of the owners —"

Some one interrupted, I believe that it was the Russian-Finn, saying: "I'll bet they," meaning the owners of our ship, "don't have to eat this old salt horse three times a day."

Riley voiced in with: "Begorra, and it's crame in their tay they are having, and divil a thimbleful do we get here."

This last expression from the Irishman pleased the cook, who brought his fist down sharply on the pork-barrel, crying: "And, men, your only salvation lies in the ballot-box."

The cook's ballot-box amused me. Who ever heard of a sailor voting? Out of ten of our crew, we had not one American citizen!

Our position at noon today was 17°.24 north latitude, — longitude 142°.10 west. The wind has been steady from the northeast for the last forty-eight hours. I am satisfied that this is the commencement of the trade-winds.

During the middle watch I was very sleepy, and decided to walk on the deck load as far forward as the mainmast, and back again, and so on. I noticed one of the crew standing against the weather main-rigging. As the night was dark, I could not make him out, and, remembering Old Charlie warning about the big Swede having it in for me, I stepped over to the fife rail and pulled out a belaying-pin, thinking that it might come in handy in case this ghost-like figure started anything. But just then he lit his pipe, and from the rays of the match I could make out the features of Old Charlie himself.

"Charlie," I said, "you scared me."

"I have been standing here thinking, sir. Have you noticed the Bo'sun flying low lately, sir?"

The "Bo'sun" Old Charlie alluded to is a tropical bird, snow-white with an exquisite tail, and flies very fast and usually very high. It is a common tradition among sailors that this beautiful bird is the embodiment of the souls of drowned sailors.

"No, Charlie," said I, "I haven't noticed them."

Taking a puff from his old pipe, and buttoning his overcoat around his neck as if expecting a squall, then looking around the horizon to make sure that we would not be interrupted by any wind-jammer:

"Yes, sir, at noon today one came near alighting on the end of the jib-boom."

"You must have mistaken it for a sea-gull," said I.

"No, sir; it was no sea-gull. I have been sailing the seas for thirty-four years, and I have seen and heard strange things."

"Well, suppose it did light on the jib-boom; it has to get a rest sometimes."

"They have their island homes and never come near a ship, unless," speaking very softly, "unless some one is going to die."

"Nonsense, Charlie. Surely you don't believe in such foolishness."

"I started to tell you some time back about an old ship I was in off the Cape of Good Hope. Maybe you remember her, she was called 'The Mud Puddler,' and Charlie continued with a grin, "she was never in the mud while I was on her."

"Yes," said I, "I remember her. She sailed from Liverpool, didn't she?"

"Yes, sir; that's her; four-masted and bark-rigged. Well, as I was saying, we left Calcutta bound for Hamburg. One night, off the Cape, it was my lookout. It was a fine night with a fresh breeze, and we were ploughing along about eight knots. I heard two bells go aft, and in that ship we had to answer all bells on the foc's'le head."

"Is it one o'clock so soon?" thought I.

"You know," speaking to me, "where the fish-tackle davit is?"

"I know where it should be," said I.

"Well, that is where I was standing." (A lookout is very important on all ships, especially at night, when they see a light or a sail they report to the officer on watch.) "As I was in a hurry to answer the bell, not wanting the mate to think I was napping, I rushed to ring it, and, standing there, sir, was a man I had never seen!"

"It was one of the crew playing a joke on you," said I.

"Oh, no, Mr. Mate, not at all, not at all. I knew every man on board of her, sir, and this man was not of this world. He had a pair of Wellington boots on, you know the kind, all leather, to just below the knee."

"Yes," said I, "I know the kind."

"He also had a sou'wester with a neat-fitting peajacket. And, sir, it was his face that frightened me. His eyes were fiery, his beard was dark and thick, with heavy, bushy eyebrows."

All this time I was getting very much interested in Old Charlie's story. "What did you do? What did you say to him?" I asked, very impatiently.

"I reached in front of him to answer the bell. He spoke very mournfully, saying: 'You shall have a visit from the Bo'sun tomorrow;' and he instantly disappeared and left me with my hand still stretched out for the bell-rope." . . .

I could smell the smoke from a cigar, and knew that the Captain was pacing the poop. I walked aft slowly, anxious to hear what happened on the bark "Mud Puddler." Sure enough, there was the Captain, walking up and down, and occasionally glancing at the compass. Evidently the ship was off her course when he came up from the cabin. He spoke to me rather harshly, saying: "Don't let these fellows," pointing to the man at the wheel, "steer her all over the ocean."

"Very well, sir. I was just forward seeing if the side-lights were burning brightly."

"Well, keep your eye on them, they are not to be trusted too long. And by the way, have the second mate get up the old spare sails in his morning watch; we have some roping and patching to do before we bend them. They are all right for this kind of weather. This breeze will carry us near the Equator."

"Very good, sir. I will have Olsen get them up."

He took one more look at the compass and went below. I went to the binnacle more to see the time than the compass. I was surprised to see that it was twenty minutes past three. I was anxious to go forward and have Charlie finish his story, but, seeing a light in the Captain's room, I was doomed to finish the watch around the man at the wheel.

My rather troubled sleep was ended by a rap at the door. It was the cook. "It has gone seven bells. Breakfast will be ready in a few minutes, sir." Dressing was easy for me. In fact, all it required was washing and putting on my cap, for in the tropics one has little use for clothes, which was indeed fortunate for me.

"Steward," said I, as I perfected my toilet, "what have you for breakfast this morning?" He hesitated before answering, and well I knew what was passing in his mind. "How does he dare to ask me what I am going to have for breakfast! I who have befriended him. What have I for breakfast indeed!"

"Tongues and sounds," said the Emancipator, very sharply.

"A breakfast fit for a king," I replied cheerfully.

The word "king" was a red flag to a bull to him. The presence of the Captain coming down the companion-way was all that saved me from the fate of all reigning monarchs.

Tongues and sounds of the Alaska codfish come pickled in brine and packed in firkins, and are sold principally to marine shipping. All that is required in the process of cooking is to freshen them overnight, boil and serve with drawn butter. They are an enviable breakfast delicacy on land and sea.

The cook, although upset by my reference to kings, lost none of the dignity of serving the byproduct of the Alaska cod. The Captain had little to say during the morning meal, and seemed worried about something.

On my leaving the table he remarked: "Get your palm and needle. I want you to work with me on the spare sails, they are in bad shape."

The spare sails were indeed much in need of repair. Where they were not worn threadbare, they had been chewed by the rats. While we were sitting side by side sewing, this afternoon, we talked of many things — ships and shipping, and foreign ports.

"Do you know," said he, "that trip that took me to South America when my wife died was going to be my last trip." He stopped sewing. "You see, she would never complain of being sick. Of course, I was away most of the time, spending about two weeks a year at home with her and the children. It was while I was home that trip, that I noticed how poorly she looked, and that cough, and realized how much she must have suffered. The doctor told me she might live for years with proper care and right climatic conditions. She and I talked it over and decided that on my return trip I would give up the sea for good, and devote my time to her and the children on a farm in Southern California. When I returned from Valparaiso and found that poor Bertha was dead, and the boys living with their aunt, it was more than I could stand."

With tears streaming from his eyes, unconscious of the vast Pacific, the ship he was in, or even the crew around him, he murmured softly to himself:

"My wife, my wife,— gone, gone." In this intense moment a ball of sewing twine rolled from his knee, and, reaching for it, he said: "Do you know that sometimes I think she is with me."

CHAPTER V

The Shark — "To Hell with Shark and Ship"

I was so overcome by the Captain's tears and his great love for his deceased wife, that I failed to hear Old Charlie calling me from the wheel until he attracted my attention by pointing over the stern.

"What is wrong?" I asked, thinking that perhaps the log line had carried away.

"A black fin on the starboard quarter, sir."

"What is that?" said the Captain, throwing the sail aside and walking aft.

"It is a shark, sir," said I, "and a black one."

Instantly all love and human kindliness left him. Jumping down onto the poop deck and looking over the rail.

"By Heavens, you are right," he cried, "he must be twenty feet long. Run to the pork barrel and get a chunk of meat while I get the shark hook."

"Aye, aye, sir." In the excitement it did not take me long to reach the cook's salt pork barrel, and grabbing about ten pounds of salt horse I was aft again in a minute. The Captain was bending a three-inch rope into a swivel on a chain. The chain is about six feet from the hook. When the shark comes down with his six rows of teeth on each jaw, it takes more than manila rope to stop him, hence the quarter-inch chain.

The Captain was very much excited. "Here, damn it. No, he will nibble it off the hook if you put it there. That is it. The center. Now over the side with it. Slack away on your line there. That is enough. Make fast."

"All fast, sir," said I.

In our excitement of the morning we had forgotten to take our observation for latitude. It was now past eight bells with the cook ringing the bell for dinner. The black fin was swimming around the salt horse, and it was easy to decide between them.

"By God, there," pointing astern, "is another one," said the Captain. "Why in blazes don't he take the bait?"

No sooner said than done. The big black fin turned over on his back and swallowed meat and hook, then righting himself and feeling grateful for so small a morsel, and starting to swim away, he found that he was fast to the end of a rope.

No one realized it more than the Captain. With a shout that could be heard all over the schooner: "Lay aft, all hands," he cried, "and lend a hand to pull in this black cannibal."

With all hands aft, including the cook,— his presence is always needed in emergencies like this,— "Get that boom tackle from off the main boom," he continued, "and you," pointing to Olsen, "get a strop from the lazarette and fasten it up in the mizzen-rigging."

"If I go down there," said Olsen, pointing to the lazarette hatch, "the cat may get out."

"To Hell with the cat," said the Captain, "this is no time to stand on technicalities. Get the strop and get it up damned lively."

Meantime the cook forgot that he was the humble dispenser of salt horse and pea soup. He who had fought the land sharks for years, he who had stood hour after hour in the sweltering sun declaiming against the crimps and other parasites of the Barbary coast, was it not befitting that he should lead the charge on this black monster of the deep?

The Ballot-Box Cook, for this is the name I gave him, was standing abaft the mizzen-rigging, with unkempt iron-gray hair waving in the wind, a greasy apron, and bare feet. His large red nose had never lost any of its cherry color, as one would expect it to, under the bleaching influence of long voyages. His large supply of extract of lemon, with its sixty per cent of alcohol, is not to be deprecated in these times, when diluted to a nicety with water and sugar.

On this particular day he had not neglected his midday tonic. Tucking his dirty apron into the belt that supported his overalls, and jumping down from the deckload to the poop deck, he exclaimed with the wildest gestures:

"Holy Moses, men, don't let him get away."

From the way that the shark was thrashing and beating the water, one would think that the three-inch rope would part from the strain at any minute.

"Stop the ship!" cried the cook.

"Stop hell," retorted the Captain.

"You will never land him," insisted the cook; "she has too much bloody way on her."

"I'll attend to this ship; I am master here," said the Captain angrily.

"Master, you are?" here discipline between master and cook was fused away into the northeast trades. The cook, coming to attention with all the dignity of a newly-made corporal, said: "Captain, I'll have you understand that I have no masters, and"— shaking his fist at the Captain, and slapping himself on the breast, "do you think that I have always been a sea-cook?"

Under other conditions the Captain would have had him put in irons, but there was now too much at stake for him to even think of such a thing. For is not time the essence of all things? With this demon of the sea dangling on the end of a sixty-foot line, every minute seemed a century with the chance that hook, meat and line might sail away into fathomless depths.

"Get to Hell forward to your galley! I will send for you when I need you"—Here the cook, with rage interrupted:

"To Hell with you, shark and ship! The American Consul shall hear about this!" With

THE SHARK

this parting shot he slouched forward to the galley.

"Here, damn you, here," continued the Captain, forgetting him on the instant. "Here, you, Nelson, put a sheep-shank in the shark-line — now hook your block in. That's the way. Hoist away on your tackle." After giving these orders he hopped up on the deck-load to direct the course of the incoming shark. With the crew pulling all their might, we could not get him in an inch.

"If we wait a little while, Captain," said Olsen, "he may drown."

"Drown be damned, who ever heard of a shark drowning? Get a snatch-block, hook it into the deck-lashing, take a line forward, and heave him in with the capstan."

Leaving the second mate with the crew to heave in the shark, I walked aft to join the Captain. While passing the galley I could hear the cook singing, "Marchons, marchons," — I knew it would be dangerous to interrupt him.

After heaving about twenty minutes the shark was alongside with the head about three feet out of water.

"Belay!" roared the Captain, "come aft, here,

a couple of you. Slip a running bowline over his head, we must not lose him. That is the way. Take a turn around the mast. All right aft. Heave away on your capstan."

As the enemy of every sailor who sails the seas came alongside, with him came the strains of the old capstan chantey:

> "Sally Brown, I love your daughter,
>   Heave, ho, roll and go,
> For seven long years I courted Sally,
>   I spent my money on Sally Brown."

Before the second verse of the aged Sally was finished, Black Fin was ours to do and dare.

"Make fast forward," shouted the Captain, "and bring your capstan bars aft. One of you get the crowbar from the donkey-room."

If there is anything in this world that a sailor loves, it is to kill a shark. We secured him safely on the deckload, for they are not to be trusted out of water, especially if one gets too near to the head or tail. This monster measured seventeen feet, six inches. With capstan bars, crowbar and sharp knives it didn't take long to take the fight out of him.

After being cut up, the choice parts were given to members of the crew, such as the backbone for a walking-stick, the gall for cleaning shoes and so forth. The eyeballs, when properly cured in the sunlight resemble oyster pearls. I took the most coveted part, the jaw, and when it was opened, it measured twenty-two inches. The Captain ordered what was left of him thrown overboard, and turning to me said, "Have the steward serve dinner."

"How about the other shark, sir?"

"Oh, we will leave him until after we eat."

After dinner there was no shark to be seen. "We have made a sad mistake," lamented the Captain. "We should not have thrown the first shark overboard. By doing that we have fed him to the second."

CHAPTER VI

The Tin-Plate Fight — One-Eyed Riley Triumphs

It was my watch below, and only one hour and a half left to sleep. Taking off my cap, I hopped into the bunk, and was just dozing off to sleep when the Cook opened the door saying: "Have you anything to read?"

"No, I have not," I replied, impatiently.

"Well," said he, unheeding, "I wish you would read this book. It is 'The Superman,' by Nietzsche. I also want you to read Karl Marx, in three volumes. Then you will understand why I hate sharks and masters." With the last remark he slammed the door behind him.

The watch from eight to twelve was wonderfully fascinating, and full of romance. A full moon hung in the clear tropical sky. The waters rippled, and the Southern Cross glimmered in the distant horizon. Occasionally a block or boom squeaked, as if to say, "I, too, lend enchantment to the night."

THE TIN-PLATE FIGHT 53

At ten-thirty the light went out in the Captain's room. I knew that, tired by the excitement of the day, it would not be long before he would be asleep. With instructions to the wheelman to keep her on her course, I went forward to see Old Charlie, and hear from him what happened next aboard the bark " Mud Puddler."

" As I was saying last night, there I stood with my hand stretched out to ring the bell, and, sir, I could not move a muscle."

" Charlie," said I, " you were just dozing and dreaming, and thought that you heard the bell aft."

" Not at all, sir, not at all. For the mate came forward cursing and swearing and telling me that if I slept again on watch he would dock me a month's pay. I have sailed under flags of many nations, sir, and never have I been caught dozing at the wheel or on the lookout."

" What about the Flying Bo'sun, did he visit your ship? "

Old Charlie was too solemn for one to think lightly of his story.

" Wait, sir, don't go too fast. At breakfast the next morning I was telling my shipmates about the strange man on the foc's'le. In describing how he looked and the clothes he wore, one old sailor seemed much interested.

"You say he wore Wellington boots and a pea-jacket? What color did you say his beard was?"

"Black and bushy," said I.

"That's very strange, very strange," said the old sailor.

One member of the crew laughed at the old man's last remark, and said: "What is strange about it? One would really believe that you thought that Charlie was awake. Ha, ha, the joke is on you."

Old John, for that was his name, pushed his hook-pot and plate over on the bench and rising very slowly to his feet said, "Shipmates, I am sixty-two years old. I have sailed the seas since I was fourteen. I want to say that the apparition that Charlie saw last night is not a joke, but a stern reality, and, shipmates, some one of us is going on the Long Voyage."

Here Charlie stopped to fill and light his pipe.

"What happened next?" I asked.

"Well, sir, in the afternoon watch I was out on the jib-boom reeving off a new jib downhaul, and, sir, as true as I stand here, there, almost within arm's length, sat the Flying Bo'sun. Three days later we ran into a storm off the Cape,— you know the short, choppy, ugly sea we get off there? It was during this storm that we lost three men, and one of them was old Sailor John. So you see I have reason to believe in coming disaster. With the Bo'sun waiting to alight, and sharks following the ship, I tell you that something is going to happen soon."

As Charlie finished his story, the man at the wheel struck one bell, a quarter to twelve. It is always customary to give the crew fifteen minutes for dressing, that when eight bells is rung the watcher may be promptly relieved. I called the second mate, got a sandwich, and went on deck again to take the distance run by the log.

While I was waiting for Olsen to relieve me Old Charlie came running aft. "They are killing each other in the foc's'le, sir."

"Who is it?" I asked.

"One-Eyed Riley and Swanson, sir."

"Who is getting the best of it?"

"Swanson, sir. He has Riley down, and is beating him over the head with a tin plate."

Looking down into the forecastle I could see Swanson stretched out with Riley standing over him, a marline-spike in his hand, cursing and swearing.

"Bad luck to you for a big squarehead. It's trying to tear me good eye out, you are. Mother of God, look at me tin plate that he bate me with, it is all crumbled in. Sure and I can't use that agin, and divil another this side of San Francisco."

"Riley," said I, "have you killed this man?"

"Begorra, sir, me intintions was well-meanin'. I broke me spike on him."

"Turn him over," I commanded, "and see if there is any life in him."

"Now, throw some water on him."

"The divil a drop will I throw on him, sir, but if you will say the word, I'll pitch him into the sea."

In a few minutes Swanson came to, terribly bruised about the head, and no more fight in him.

"Riley," said I, "you beat this man, now you must bandage him up and take care of him."

"Ah, sure, sir; it's murdher you'd be after

wantin' me to do and it's bandage him up you want. Heavenly Father, with me new tin plate all spoiled, what in the divil am I going to ate off of?"

"Eight bells!" sang out the man on the lookout. It was Swanson's lookout watch, and the Finn's wheel.

"Riley, you will have to keep the Swede's lookout this watch. He is dazed and stupid from the beating you gave him. There is danger of him walking overboard."

Swanson crawled over to the bench as if in terrible pain, muttering: "I will get this Irish dog, and when I do, look out, I will kill him."

The other members of the watch below were too busy dressing to pay much attention to the fight, but one could see that they were proud of Riley's work.

"Ha, ha, an' it's kill me you would, me fine bucko, an' sure you might if I had no eyes in me head. You dirty baste. Let me finish him, sir."

"Riley," said I, severely, "get up on deck, and relieve the man on the lookout, or I will place you both in irons."

Riley went on duty very reluctantly, saying,

"Begorra, sir, and it's sorry you'll be for not letting me finish him."

"Swanson," I said, "you will be all right in the morning. You have a few bad bumps on your head, but a hard and tough man like you should not mind that.

I left him grumbling and whining and swearing vengeance, saying to himself: "By Jiminy, I get even mit dem all."

On the forecastle head Riley was pacing up and down, evidently very happy and pleased with the night's work. He was humming an old ditty, and sometimes breaking out singing:

> "Blow you winds while sails are spreading,
>   Carry me cheerily o'er the sea.
> I'll go back, de dom, de dido,
>   To my sweetheart in the old countree."

In the cabin the Captain was looking through the nautical almanack to find a star that was crossing our meridian.

"You know," speaking to me, "we must not allow sharks nor anything else to interfere with the progress of the ship. I want to cross the Equator about in 150° west. I believe that I shall have to keep her a little to the westward now. Ah, here I have it, the star Draconis, it crosses our meridian at 1 hr. 15 min. Just give me your latitude by dead reckoning."

"Here you are, sir," handing him the latitude. "With this moderate breeze she has made 110 miles since noon today."

"It looks," said he, "as if she were going to beat her last trip to the Equator. But, of course, there's the doldrums. One can never tell. Sometimes a ship will run through and into the southeast trades, and escape the doldrums. But that seldom happens to me."

The next few days were spent sewing sails, the crew rattling her down, cleaning brass-work and chipping iron rust from the anchor chain. A ship is like a farm, there is always work to be done, and a sailor must never be idle. It is the mate's duty to find work to keep them going. A mate's ability is usually measured by the amount of work that he gets out of the crew, especially when she sails into her home port.

There the owners come aboard, and if they do not wring their hands, and tear their hair, and sometimes tramp on their hats or caps, the mate is indeed to be complimented. They will sometimes walk up to you and say:

"Well, you had a fine voyage, I see," looking around at the masts, and yards, and paint-work. "Do you smoke? Here is a very fine cigar, three for a dollar." (More often it is three for ten cents.)

I remember the old barque "Jinney Thompson." We were three weeks overdue. When we finally arrived the owner was there on the dock and fired every man aboard her. It seems that every day for three weeks he had never failed to make his appearance at the wharf. On this day while the tug-boat was docking us there he stood, white with rage.

"Get off my ship, you damned pirates, every man, woman and child of you! To think that I should have lost one hundred and fifty dollars on this trip. Get off, damn you, get off!"

CHAPTER VII

In Which the Captain Wounds His Hand

"No, sir, he won't stay down there," said the cook. "He caught a flying-fish the other night; it lit on the deck forward. Since then he just sits in the main rigging watching. When I get near him he runs up aloft."

"I must tell the mate," said the Captain, "to move the flour into the spare room. Those damned rats will eat us out yet. Why don't you tie Toby with the stores?"

"I can't, sir, he won't let me near enough."

This conversation was going on in the cabin while I was trying to read Henry George. I went to sleep wondering how a single tax could be applied to city property. I was not asleep long before I was awakened by loud tapping on my door. "Come in," said I. The door opened. There stood the Captain, pale and excited.

"Would you mind tying up this hand for me? I stuck a marline spike through here," pointing to the fleshy part between the thumb and forefinger of the right hand.

"Just one minute, sir, I'll get some hot water."

Fortunately there was hot water in the galley.

"There you are, sir, put your hand in the bucket. No, it is not too hot. There, see, I hold my hand in it."

Satisfied that there was no danger of cooking it, he pulled the rag off, and thrust his hand into the bucket. I noticed that there was no blood to speak of. I said, "Captain, did the spike go through your hand?"

"Hell, yes, man, about three inches."

I suggested many remedies, such as washing it with saline solution and bandaging with oakum and so on. But he would have none of them, and insisted on having the rag tied around, assuring me that it would be well in a day or so. He kept on deck most of the first watch, but was evidently in great pain.

"I think that we are running into the doldrums from the look of those clouds to the eastward," said he.

"We have one thing in our favor," I replied;

"we should have a three-knot current to the southward according to the pilot chart."

"You should not rely on what those fellows in Washington put onto paper. If you do you will never get anywhere."

At five o'clock in the morning it was raining. There is no place in the world where it rains as it does around the Equator; it seems as if the celestial sluice-gates had gotten beyond control. We were becalmed, and in the doldrums, with not a breath of air. Usually this lasts for five or six days.

During this time every one on board is very busy, catching water, filling barrels, washing clothes, and working ship. The latter work is hard on the crew, for you are always trimming ship for every puff of wind that comes along. Pity the weak-kneed mate in the doldrums. There are times when you tack and wear, and boxhaul ship every fifteen minutes. The crew resent this kind of work, and while doing it they curse and swear, and will do the opposite to what they are told.

Here is where the old-school mate comes in.

Obey orders. He sees that they do obey. Lazy sailors breed discontent, and discipline must be stern. If a member of the crew happens to be idle, he must by no means appear to be. He must at least act very seriously, and look to windward, as if beckoning for a breeze. There is an old saying among sailing-ship-men:

"When the wind is fair the money comes in over the stern,
When the wind is ahead the money comes in over the bow."

so a sailor must never show that the unfavorable weather is making pay for him. He must never whistle a tune, nor sing a song, but he is privileged at all times during a calm to whistle as if he were calling a dog, for if you don't get wind with the dog-whistling, you are not to blame. I have seen captains standing for hours whistling for wind. Pity the man who would smile or crack a joke on so serious an occasion. One captain I was with, after whistling off and on all day without avail, threw three of his hats overboard, one after the other, crying in rage, " There, now, damn you, give us a gale."

The wise mate knows his place in trying times like these. He never goes aft, thereby avoiding serious discussions. He always makes it his business to be very busy in the forepart of the ship. The worst time for him is meal-time. It is not uncommon to finish eating without a word being spoken. The cook is not exempt. Should the captain count more than ten raisins in the bread-pudding, look out for a squall!"

At breakfast I ate alone. The Captain was walking around in his room.

"How is your hand, sir?" I inquired.

"It is very painful. I have just been washing it with a little carbolic acid I found in a drawer."

"I have taken off staysails, topsails and inner and outer jib, sir."

He did not answer, but shut his door with a slam. I was worried about his condition, but was helpless to do anything for him. He was the stubborn type, with tight lips, and projecting cheek-bones. He believed that what he could not do for himself no other could do for him. I think that this applied only to strangers. As captain of a ship you are always dealing with new faces, and never have much confidence in any one. For instance if, in taking the altitude of the sun or a star, his reckoning should differ from yours by a mile or so, you would always be wrong. The same with longitude by chronometer in time.

The loneliness of the sea must be responsible for this. And yet in their home life, they are ruled and dominated by their wives and children. I remember one old captain I sailed with in the China Seas. Fight? He loved it, ashore and afloat, and was very proud of his ability, claiming that he never took the count. The latter I know to be true. We left ports while I was sailing with him, where much furniture was easily adaptable for firewood.

When in the home port where his wife was, if he had spent more than she allowed him, I would have to make up the difference. She would come down to the ship and say: "Herman, come here, I want you to do so and so." He would look at me, but never ashamed, and say, "Well, what in Hell can I do?"

"But, Captain, I want your advice on so and so."

"Never mind now," he would say, "till I steer her away. You know she don't like you too well anyhow. She heard all about the fight we had in Yokohama with the rickshaw men." Away they would go, arm in arm, a very happy couple.

CHAPTER VIII

THE BO'SUN LIGHTS — THE CAPTAIN'S DEATH

I was so worried about the Captain that I had no desire to sleep during the forenoon watch. About eleven o'clock he came to my room saying:

"I can't stand this pain, it is driving me wild. You take charge of the ship. Take every possible advantage you can, until we run out of the doldrums. Here are charts covering the South Sea Isles, and here," pointing to a small box, "is the Manifest, and Bill of Health." While looking at the latter I came into contact with his right hand. I was surprised to find that he was burning with fever.

"Captain, may I look at your hand?"

He eyed me with the same suspicion as when I was suggesting treatments on the previous day. But the stubborn nature of him was giving way to a feeling of friendship and sympathy, a sympathy so noticeable in all living creatures when their material existence is in danger.

THE BO'SUN LIGHTS

"Yes, you can look at it, if it will do you any good," holding the hand out for me to take the bandage off. "I don't mind the hand so much as I do this lump under my arm, it is so painful."

With the bandage off I was horrified to see the condition of the wound. It was turning black, and a fiery red stripe ran up the arm. He must have guessed what was going on in my mind.

"Yes," said he, "it is blood-poisoning, and a damned bad case. Don't tell me what to do for it. I have tried everything I can think of to prevent this condition."

"Let us cut it open and keep it in hot water," said I.

"Tie it up again," he replied angrily, "you are only adding insult to injury." He turned to his wife's picture which hung at the head of the bed, saying, "You understand, you understand. We may soon sail away through the silvery seas to our Land of the Midnight Sun."

I went on deck thoroughly alarmed at the Captain's condition and aware that, unless a miracle should happen within the next forty-eight hours, he would be dead of septicæmia.

We were still becalmed;—not a breath to curl the blue roll. With booms and sails swinging and wailing as she rolled and pitched in the trough of the sea, the angry gods of the Celestial World belched forth their wrath in thunder and lightning. This, coupled with the condition of the Captain, made me feel, as never before, the utter lonesomeness of the sea. It was useless, with the clouded skies, to try to get a position of the ship for drift. She had made no progress by log for twenty hours. I was anxious to know the course and speed of the current.

In going forward to see what the crew was doing, I met Olsen coming aft, holding a wet rag over his eye.

He said, "I have had trouble with Swanson, he refuses to work ship. He thinks it is not necessary to tack and boxhaul, he wants to wait for the wind."

Olsen had the real thing, if black eyes count in the performance of one's duty.

"Are you afraid of him?" said I. "If you are, keep away from him. You will only spoil him, and make him believe that he is running the ship. Here," and I pulled a belaying-pin out from the fife-rail, "Go forward and work this on him."

"No," said Olsen, "he is too big and strong for me. He told me that there is no one on board big and strong enough to make *him* work. I understand that he almost killed a mate named Larsen—"

Here the cook interrupted, saying: "Mr. Mate, the Captain wants you in the cabin."

"Do you want me, sir?"

"Yes, this pain is killing me, killing me, don't you realize how I am suffering? Why did you leave me? Why don't you do something to relieve me of this burning Hell?"

I did realize that the poison was general, and that he was becoming delirious. The unshaven face, the ruffled hair, the dry parched lips, the wild staring. It was plain that for him Valhalla lay in the offing.

"Yes, Captain," said I, "you are suffering, but strong men like you must be brave. You, who for years weathered the storms of Seven Seas, must now keep off the lee shore. The wind will soon be off the land. Then ho! for the ocean deep."

"You are very kind," he said, collecting himself to try to cheer me up, "but it is no use. For I can see the lee shore with its submerged and dangerous reefs, I can hear the billows roar, and watch the thunderous sea pour its defiance on the ragged crags of granite. Yes, I am drifting, drifting there."

After cutting open the hand and arm, and bathing in salt solution, he felt somewhat relieved, and decided that he would try to sleep. Leaving him in charge of the cook, with instructions to keep him in bed, I went on deck with a heavy heart, realizing that soon I should be responsible for the crew and cargo.

Old Charlie was at the wheel. "How is the Captain, sir?"

"He is a very sick man, Charlie."

"Look, look," he cried, "there he comes, lower and lower," and he pointed to the maintopmast truck. "Great Heavens, he is going to alight! Yes, yes; there he sits," and there, sure enough, sat the most beautiful bird in the tropics, the Flying Bo'sun.

I spent the afternoon sitting with the Captain, who was still sleeping. At five o'clock I tried to arouse him, but found that he had lapsed into a state of coma. I left Olsen and the cook looking after him while I went to see to the ship.

About eleven o'clock I felt very sleepy, having then been without sleep for eighteen hours. In order to keep awake, I decided to walk on the deck-load until Olsen relieved me. It was while thus walking that I went asleep, and fell, or walked, overboard.

The deck-load of lumber is always stowed with the shear of the ship and flush with the sides or bulwarks. There is no rail or lifeline, and hence the sudden plunge. Coming to the surface I was very much awake, and swimming to the chain plates, I easily pulled myself out of the water, and into the rigging, and up onto the deck. While I was wringing out my pants, Old Charlie came creeping aft, saying: " Mr. Mate, something is going to happen from his visit today."

" To Hell with your Flying Bo'sun," I snapped, " you are always predicting death and ghosts and so on."

I was sorry that I had spoken to the old sailor this way, but after falling fifteen feet into the ocean, and just, by the chance of a calm, saving my life, I was in no mood to tolerate the re-incarnated souls of drowned sailors that were living in Old Charlie's Flying Bo'sun.

Charlie, much distressed at having the omens he loved so dearly so lightly disregarded, slunk away in the shadow of the mainsail.

Riley, the man on the lookout, was true to his trust, and no object in the hazy horizon would escape the vigilance of his squinty left eye. Evidently he was not carried away by the supernatural things of life, but very much in the material, judging from his song:

"Better days are coming to reward us for our woe,
And we'll all go back to Ireland when the landlords
    go."

When Olsen relieved me on deck, I took his place with the Captain, who, although unconscious, was still hanging to the delicately spun threads of life. As I was sponging the dry and parched lips, I glanced at the picture of her whom he loved so well. How beautiful it would be, if it should come to pass as he believed, and she should pilot him away in their astral ship to the shades of Valhalla!

While my thoughts ran thus, I was suddenly conscious of a desert stillness. Then creaking booms gave way to a gentle lullaby. The ship no longer rolled and pitched in the trough of the sea. Everything below was peaceful and calm. I could hear Olsen calling:

"Slack away on the boom-tackle, and haul in on your spanker-sheet!"

I knew then that at last we had the long-looked-for southeast trade-winds. With the wind came taut sheets and steady booms, and on the face of the dead Captain there was a smile as if saying:

"Away with you to the tall green palms!"

CHAPTER IX

THE SHOWDOWN — SWANSON TAKES THE COUNT

I dimmed the swivel light in the Captain's room, locked the door and went on deck. Above, there was a fair breeze, and the sky was clear and glittering with millions of stars.

"What course are you steering?" said I to the man at the wheel.

"South-southwest, sir."

"Let her go off to southwest." I was anxious to take advantage of the wind by getting all sail on her.

"Where is the second mate?"

"He is forward, sir, setting the jibs."

Going forward, I shouted to Olsen: "Get the topsails and staysails on her as fast as you can."

"Aye, aye, sir. I am short-handed; Swanson refuses to come on deck. I sent Russian-Finn John down to tell him that we had a fine breeze, and wanted him to come up and trim ship. Do you know, sir, he kicked him out of the fo'c'sle?"

I took stock of myself. I was twenty-four years old, and weighed one hundred and eighty pounds. The big brute in the forecastle, refusing to work, whipping the second mate, and kicking his shipmates about, was getting too much for me. I made up my mind that there would be two dead captains or one damned live one.

Going aft to my room, I got a pair of canvas slippers that I had made, for with this brute I should be handicapped in bare feet. With the slippers on, and overalls well cinched up around me, I went to the forecastle, past Olsen, who was sheeting home the fore-topsail.

Calling down the forecastle, I said: "Swanson, come on deck." When he appeared: "I suppose you know that you are guilty of a crime on the high seas?"

He answered me back, saying: "I tank about it," and took his stand obstinately at the foot of the ladder.

The anger and passion of thousands of years was upon me. I forgot the ship, forgot the dead captain. I skidded down the scuttle-hatch into the forecastle, where he stood, awaiting me with a large sheath-knife in his hand.

"Are you going on deck?" I shouted.

"You ——, ——, ——," flourishing the knife; "kap avay from me, I kill you!"

I noticed an oilskin coat hanging on the bulkhead. I must say that my mind was working overtime. My height was five feet eleven, and he towered above me like a giant. I was aware of the powerful legs and arms of this brute, conveying the suggestion of second money to me. If I were to trim this gorilla, it would require tact and skill. Otherwise I felt that the dead Captain would not have much start on me. He took a step toward me, saying:

"You get on deck damn quick, or by Jiminy I cut your heart out!"

Quick as a flash I seized the oilskin coat. As he raised his arm to stab me I threw it over his head and arm, then jumped for him. After some minutes' hard work I succeeded in wresting the knife from him, but not without marks on my legs, arms and hands. The forecastle was so small it was hard to do much real fighting. It was more rough and tumble, and this kind of a battle favored the Swede.

While slashing with the knife, he cut the belt that held up my overalls. I was handicapped by these hanging around my feet, but fortunately landed a right on his jaw, which sent him falling into his bunk. This gave me a chance to kick free from the pants, and in so doing I kicked one of the canvas shoes off. I can't remember when I lost the shirt, but what was left of it was lying by the bench. He pulled himself from the bunk saying, "I tank I go on deck."

"Well," thought I, "there is not much fight in him after all."

It was about twelve feet from the forecastle to the deck. When he reached the deck I started up after him. When my head was even with the deck, he stepped from behind the scuttle and kicked me in the forehead, knocking me back to the forecastle. Had he followed up the blow I should have indeed joined the dead Captain.

But no, he thought that he had finished me for good.

When I came to, I could hear strange noises around me. Some one was washing my face, and saying: "And begorra, it is far from being finished you are, me good man." It was Riley.

Old Charlie voiced in, saying: "That is a bad cut on his forehead."

Riley had no use for pessimists. "Ah, go wan with you, sure an it is only a scratch he has. Now when I had me eye knocked out—"

Here I got upon my feet, dazed, but with no broken bones. "Where is Swanson?"

"He is aft by the mainmast, sur, and be Hivins, it is a sight he is, sur."

"Riley," said I, "come on deck and throw a few buckets of salt water on me." There is nothing so invigorating as salt water when one is exhausted.

After the bath, with its salty sting in my cuts and scratches, I was ready for the cur again. He saw me coming up on the deck-load, and straightened up as if he thought that there was still some fight left in me. I noticed that he had a wooden belaying-pin in his hand. I took my cue from that.

Stalling that I was all in, and crawling aft to my room, I gave him this impression until I was abreast of him, and then I was on him with a vengeance. I snatched the pin from him, and finished him in a hurry. When he cried for mercy, and promised that he would work, and work with a will, I decided that he had had as good a trimming as I could give him, and let him up.

"Now, I want you to stay on deck, and work until I tell you that you can have a watch below."

Calling all hands, I said, "Men, our Captain died during the middle watch. We will bury him at nine o'clock this morning."

With the surprised and solemn look of the crew as they heard my announcement, was mingled no mirth at my scant attire of one canvas shoe. That was lost in their sympathy for him who was taking the long sleep, and I doubt if they noticed it at all.

Death on board a ship creates a hushed stillness. Amongst the crew Old Charlie looked up at the mast as if expecting another Bo'sun to appear. He seemed satisfied with his predictions. But Riley took a different view.

"Mother of God! It's fighting there has been going on with the poor dead Captain laying aft there. Be Heavens, sir," pointing, "it's bad luck we will be having for carrying on like this in the presence iv th' dead."

Sending him after my overalls and shoe, I went to my room to look myself over. My eyes were black, face cut, arms, hands and body cut and scratched, and worst of all, was my forehead where the brute had kicked me. I still carry this scar. I was somewhat alarmed with these open wounds, and knew that I must be careful of handling the Captain.

Hot breakfast, with its steaming coffee, did much to revive me, and for the second time I was aware that the Socialist cook was a friend in need.

CHAPTER X

BURIAL AT SEA — AT WHICH RILEY OFFICIATES

At eight o'clock I called Riley and Old Charlie aft to the cabin. "Riley," said I, opening the door to the Captain's room, "I want you and Charlie to sew the Captain's body in this tarpaulin, while I go and find something to sink it with. Roll him over towards the partition, then roll him back onto the hatch-cover, then gather it in at both ends."

"Aye, aye, sir, and shure it is meself that has sewed many av thim up."

In the boatswain's locker I found plenty of old chain bolts and shackles. I had one of the crew carry them to the weather main rigging. While going down the companion-way to see how Riley and Charlie were getting along with their sewing, I thought, by a sudden noise, that they had begun to quarrel.

"Where the divil did you ever sew up a dead man?" came in Riley's voice, and "Damn you, pull that flap down over his face." Then I could hear boots and glasses being thrown around. "Get out of here, you black divil, it's eating your master you would be doing, pss-cat, pss-cat, you dirty, hungry-looking tiger!"

Then all was still for a few seconds. Then Old Charlie's voice saying, "Mike Riley, this is a terrible calamity that has happened to us, the loss of our captain. And Riley, this is not all. I am afraid there will be more."

"Ah, go wan wit your platting," said Riley, "Pull the seam tight around his neck. That is the way. Now sew it with a herring-bone stitch. Hould on a minute, Charlie, till I get me last look at him. Faith, and be my sowl, he wasn't a very bad-looking man."

Here I walked into the room, saying: "When you are finished I will get you more help to carry him on deck. But leave a place open at the head so that we can put the weights in."

"Sinking him by the head is it you are, sir? Glory be to God, don't do that. Let him go down feet first, sir. Be Hivins, if you put him down be the head we will have the divil's own luck! I remember wan time on the auld lime-juicer

'King of the Seas,' the second mate died. We weighed him down by the head — begob, and it wasn't a week till ivery man av us had the scurvy."

"Riley," I laughed, "you are a very superstitious man."

"It's you that are mistaken, sir. Sure an I'm annything but that, sir."

The cook interrupted us to ask if he could help in any way. I told him to help Charlie and Riley carry the body up on deck. Riley at once took command. "Charlie, you take the head, I will take the feet, and, Steward, you can help in the middle. Are you all ready? Up wit him, then,— be Hivins isn't he heavy?"

Charlie started towards the door so as to take the body out head first. Riley promptly objected to this move, and propped the feet on the edge of the berth while he asserted his authority.

"And it's take him out be the head ye'd be after doing? Where in blazes did you come from? Oh, you poor auld divil you! Who ever heard of takin' a corpse out head first. Turn him around, bad luck to you, with his feet out. Sure, an it's walk out on his feet he would, if he were on thim. Niver do that, Charlie, me boy, if ye want to prosper in this life."

We pulled two planks from the deckload, and spiked cross-pieces on, while Riley supervised the weighing-down. Then all was ready to commit the body to the deep blue sea.

While the second mate was back-filling the foresail and hauling the main-jib to windward, to stop the ship for sea-burial, I fell to thinking of our Captain. Here he was, in the prime of life, about to be cast into the sea. No one to love him, no one to care, none but the rough if kindly hands of sailors to guide him to his resting-place. As I glanced around the horizon, and the broad expanse of the Pacific, I was overcome by loneliness. Ships might come and ships might go, and still there would be no sign of his last resting-place, no chance to pay respects to the upright seaman, the devoted husband and father. The silent ocean currents, responsible to no one, would be drifting him hither and thither.

The last few days and the terrible fight were telling upon me.

I was astonished to look around and find that

I was alone with the dead. The only other person on deck was Broken-Nosed Pete at the wheel.

I went forward and sung out: "Come forward, some of you, and lend a hand here."

"Aye, aye, sir; we are coming," answered Riley's brogue.

There was something about Riley, in his simple seriousness and appeal to my humor, that was a great help to me just now. They came aft, every one of them, in their best clothes, with shined and squeaky shoes, looking very solemn. "Here," said I, "take a hand and shove the planks out so that the body will clear the bulwark rail when she rolls to windward." I was about to give the order to tip the plank, when I was interrupted by Riley saying excitedly: "Lord God, sir, aren't you going to say something over him?"

"Riley," I said as the crew gathered around, "I have nothing to say, except that I commit this body to the sea. Up with the plank."

"Hould on, hould on," cried Riley in despair. "Sure I wouldn't send a dog over like that! I will read the Litany of the Blissed Virgin Mary, and it don't make a damned bit av diffrunce whether he belaves it or not. Hould on, me boy, till I get my prayer book."

Riley returned from the forecastle cursing and swearing.

"Howly Mother av Moses, they have ate the Litany out av me prayer-book, and the poor sowl about to be throwed overboard."

"What is the matter, Riley?" I asked.

"Ah, the dirty divils! The rats has made a nest av me Holy Prayer-book!"

"Sanctified rats —" I was beginning profanely, when fortunately the cook interrupted me.

"What good will a prayer-book do him now? Your prayer-books, and flowers and beautiful coffins are only advertisements of ignorance. The man of thought today throws those primitive things away, or sends them back to the savages. You men will in time come to believe in a Creative Power of Organization, or a Material Force, but in your present state of ignorance you are carried away by a supernatural power destined for the poor and helpless."

While the cook was talking Riley was taking off his coat, and rolling up his sleeves. "It is poor and helpless we are, are we? You durty, fat, Dutch hound. Take back what you were saying," as he grabbed him by the neck, "or be me sowl it's over you go before the Owld Man. It is ignorant we are, and savages we are. Take that," hitting him on the jaw. "Be Hivins and I'll not sail wit a heathen. Come on, me boys. Over wit him."

"Here, Riley," I said, "this must stop. Don't you know that you are in the presence of the dead? Every one has the privilege of believing what he wants to."

"He has that, sir, but begorra, he wants to keep it to himself."

"Men," said I, "we will raise the plank. While we are doing it let us sing, 'Nearer, my God, to Thee.'"

While we were singing the beautiful hymn, the old ship we loved so well seemed to feel this solemn occasion. Although held in irons by having her sails aback, she did salute to her former captain by some strange freak of the sea, coming up in the wind, and shaking her sails.

Before we finished the singing the cook was

leading in a rich tenor voice, and by the time that the last sound had died away, our Captain had slid off into the deep.

* * * *

" Let go your main jib to windward, haul in the fore-boom sheet." To the man at the wheel, " Let her go off to her course again."

CHAPTER XI

ASTRAL INFLUENCE — THE CREW'S VERSION OF THE UNKNOWN

With these orders the crew, although silent and solemn, went about their various duties in their shiny and squeaky shoes, the only remaining sign of what had come to pass.

I told the steward to throw all of the Captain's clothing overboard. He protested, saying, "Surely, sir, you won't destroy his blankets?"

"Oh, yes, Steward, there are enough germs in those blankets to destroy all of Coxey's Army."

This mention of Coxey's Army was a mistake indeed. He changed at once from the comparative refinement that the hymn had wrought in him, to the fiery rage of the soap-box orator.

"They were the men," he thundered, "who make life possible for you and me. Otherwise we should be ground in the mill of the lust and greed of capitalism."

He started to lead off on the subject of equal distribution, when I interrupted:

"Steward, this is no place to expound your theories of Socialism. You have done much harm since you came aboard this ship. Here," pointing to Swanson, who was slowly recovering from his battle for supremacy, "is a man who was led to believe from listening to your radical doctrines that work was not a necessary element in his life. Living in your world of thought, he gained the impression that refusing to work and disobeying orders was a perfectly natural thing to do. Now let me impress you with this thought — while you are aboard this ship with me, I'll not tolerate any more of your ill-advised teachings to the crew."

Later, while he was throwing the Captain's bedding overboard, I could hear him say:

". . . To the vile dust from whence they sprung,
Unwept, unhonored and unsung."

December 20th, 1898. Our position of ship at noon today was four miles north latitude, longitude 147° 19" west. In looking over the chart I found that the course had been laid out by the Captain before his death. Although now seventy miles to the eastward of it, I decided with favorable winds to follow this line to the South Sea Isles.

It was while doing this work that I fell to pondering my responsibilities to the owners, the crew and the consignees. We were carrying about five hundred thousand feet of select lumber to Suva, Fiji Islands. I had never visited these islands, but had read of their submerged reefs and tricky currents. Up to this time I had taken my responsibilities negatively, being of the age when one is not taken seriously, and I must say being rather inclined to lean on those higher up. This latter is, I believe, very destructive to one's self-confidence and determination, those qualities so necessary in fitting one for leadership both by land and sea.

In cleaning up the Captain's cabin I was deeply impressed with his remarkable sense of order. His best clothes were lashed to a partition to keep from chafing by the roll of the ship. The ash-tray was fastened to the floor across the room and opposite the bed, and there also stood tobacco, matches, cigars and spittoon. When using these things he would have to get up and move clear across the room from his writing-desk or bed, which seemed out of place for a sailor-man.

(Captains whom I sailed with usually disregarded any and all sense of order, preferring not to interfere with the laws of gravity, particularly when chewing tobacco. But if these same white shirts happened to leave the hand of the sailor who washed them with any remnant of stain, His Majesty could be heard swearing all over the ship.)

For the past three days everything has been going beautifully, with the wind free and fair. We are clipping it off at ten knots an hour.

To-night I noticed that the man at the wheel acted rather queerly, and was not steering at all well. The men looked continually from left to right, acting as if they feared that some one was going to strike them.

It was during the middle watch that I heard a conversation in the forecastle between Riley, Old Charlie and Broken-Nosed Pete. Charlie was trying to convince Pete by saying:

"You may not understand, but it is true, none the less. Look at me in the 'Mud Puddler.'"

The suspense of this argument was evidently getting on Riley's nerves. He interrupted with,

"Damn it all, man, I tell you he is back on the ship. Haven't we all heard him prancing around in his room? Upon my sowl, I have felt him looking into the compass. Oh, be Hivins, me good man, you will see him soon enough."

Here Old Charlie once more took the floor. "Riley," said he, "I believe that he has come back to warn us of some danger."

"Divil a bit av danger we will be having." This with bravado.

"You know he may have come back to find his knife. You remember when you sewed him up you found it in his bed."

"Ah, go wan, you durty ape, didn't I throw it overboard with him?"

"It may be he wants to talk with some one."

"Be Hivins, shure I don't want to talk wit him. Why sure'n I don't know the man at all. I niver shpoke a wurd to him on this ship."

"Well, it does seem that he is trying to manifest himself to you more than to any one on this ship. Why not ask him if you can help him in any way?" Evidently this conversation was getting too creepy for Riley for he changed the subject, declaring with great feeling that he had never seen a more beautiful night, and so near Christmas too.

But Charlie was not to be put off that way.

"Riley," he said, "can't you feel him around here at this moment?"

"Ah, go wan, to Hell wit you, sure'n you will have him keepin' the lookout wit you the next we hear."

I was so much interested in what I had heard that I jumped up onto the forecastle head. I came upon them so suddenly that Riley jumped back exclaiming, "Hivinly Father, and what is this?"

He seemed greatly relieved when I spoke and said artfully:

"Isn't this a beautiful night? See how large and bright those stars are there," pointing to the Southern Cross. "You men seem to have some secret about this ship,— what is it?" I continued, as my remark met with no response.

Old Charlie cleared his throat, and, looking towards Riley as if for an approval, said solemnly: "Things are not as they should be aft."

"What is it? Aren't you being treated well? Aren't you getting enough to eat?"

ASTRAL INFLUENCE 97

"On, it isn't that at all, sir," broke in Riley.

"Hold on, Riley, let me explain," and Old Charlie once more cleared his throat.

"As I was saying, we believe that the ghost of the Captain is back on board," tapping the deck with his foot.

I felt that a word of encouragement was necessary if I expected to be let in on the mystery. "Well," said I, "that is nothing. Men who have been taken suddenly out of this life may perhaps have left some important business unfinished, and the most natural thing in the world is for them to find some one whom they can converse with."

"That's just what I was telling Riley, sir, that very same thing, and you know Riley seems to have more influence with him than any one so far."

"Influence is it?" said Riley, "and shure, sir, he is a stranger intirely to me."

"Tell me about it, Riley."

"It's a damned strange thing, sir. Well, it was me watch from ten to twelve. I was just after striking six bells, when I takes a chew of me tobacco, and ses I to myself I had better be careful where I spit around here. I know, sir, you don't like tobacco juice on the paint-work. Reaching down to locate the spit-box to make sure that I could do it daycently, be me sowl, sur, something flipped by me. Shtraitening up, ses I to meself, ses I, ' Be Hivins, and it must be the blood running to me head.' I took a look at the compass, and she was one point to windward of her course. You were forward, sir, taking a pull on the forestaysail-halyards, and I ses to meself, 'Sure an if he comes aft and catches me with her off her course he will flail me like he did the big Swede.' Ah, an shure it is the fine bye he is now. There's the Squarehead so rejuced he even offers to wash me tin plate for me. Well, I got her back on her course, when all of a sudden I heard the divil's own noise in the Captain's room. Ses I to myself, ses I, ' Mike Riley, don't be a damned fool and belave iverything you hear.' But look as I would I could not keep my eyes from the window of the Captain's room, whin lo and behold, I got a glimpse of his face looking out at me. ' Hivenly Father,' ses I, ' give me strenk and faith in yous to finish me watch.' Glory be to God, sir, I lost me head, and it's hard up wit me helm I was doing, when you shouted, 'Where in Hell are you going with her?' Be Hivins, and I was going straight back with her."

During this story Broken-Nosed Pete kept edging closer, seemingly impressed, and about to become a convert to Riley's sincerity, while Old Charlie was just revelling in the details of the apparition, and at times, thinking that Riley was not doing justice to his subject in creating the proper amount of enthusiasm, would interrupt by saying, "There you are now. Just as I was saying. One couldn't expect anything else," — and so forth.

These remarks seemed to resolve any doubts that may have existed in Riley's mind of the genuineness of the face at the window.

CHAPTER XII

THE COOK'S WATCH — MATERIALISM VERSUS ASTRALISM

I had the key to the Captain's room in my pocket and knew that no one was in there, but Riley's story had taken such a serious trend that I decided to withhold the news from them.

"Well, Riley," I said carelessly, "you are easily frightened, when Toby can scare you like this."

Here they all jumped toward me, and started to talk at once. Charlie, calling for order, decided that now was the time to fix me forever. He introduced Broken-Nosed Pete, who had always been inclined to be skeptical, to put the finishing touches on Riley's story.

Pete, I may state, when he was rational, was unaffected in his speech by the rather unusual list of his nose. But tonight, moved by powerful feelings, he threw convention to the winds, and spoke in loud nasal tones, and with gestures befitting an orator.

"Go on," said Charlie, pushing him forward, "tell him, Pete."

"I had just called the watch below," he began, "and was taking my smoke and a bite of lunch. By that time it was eight bells. I was pulling down my blankets about to turn in, when I sees Riley coming down the scuttle with his cap in his hand and very warm looking. 'Is Toby in here?' ses Riley. 'He is,' ses I. 'He is over in Russian-Finn John's bunk.' 'Holy Mother of God,' ses Riley, 'get me a drink of water, 'tis fainting I am.' 'What's wrong, Riley?' I asks. 'Oh, be Hivins,' ses he, 'I have made the mistake of me life by ever shipping on this dirty old graveyard.' As for the rest, sir, you have heard it from Riley."

"Was Riley scared when he came into the forecastle?" I asked.

"Yes, sir, he swore horribly, and threatened to kill anybody who put out the light."

"Well, we will all have some fun catching this ghost of yours. I will give an extra day's leave in Suva to the man who helps me. What do you say to that, men?" Charlie volunteered willingly. Pete was rather shy.

"Riley, let us hear from you."

"What is it you want us to do, sir?"

"I want each of you to take one hour watches in the Captain's room from twelve to four." This was too much for Riley.

"Be Hivins, sir, if ye offered me a year's leaf in a Turkish Harem to stay five minutes in the auld haunted room, I wouldn't take it, for as sure as me name is Michael Dennis Riley he is rummaging around there."

The news of the ghost soon spread over the ship, and formed the sole topic of conversation of the crew. Even the second mate, whom I thought immune, was going around the decks looking bewildered, as if anticipating the immediate destruction of ship and crew.

The Socialist cook was much interested in our astral visitor, and I thought how happy it would make him to sail away on the wings of a new law that would revolutionize both physics and chemistry.

"Yes," he said, "you can trust me to keep watch from twelve to two tonight in the Captain's room. I am very much pleased indeed to have the opportunity. I have for years been fighting the mechanical and cheap manifestations of mediums and seers." He picked up his apron and wiped his mouth, to interrupt the line of march of tobacco juice which, having broken the barriers, was slowly wending its way down his chin.

"Let me tell you," he said. "A material law gives us life. The same law takes it away. All material life," stamping the deck, "ends here. From the clay there is no redemption."

At one o'clock in the morning the cook called me.

"What do you want, Steward?" said I.

"There is something in the Captain's room. Something I can't understand. When I am in the room with the light out, I am conscious of some one with me. And yet when I turn on the light that feeling leaves me. Then when I turn out the light and lock the door and sit here by the dining-table I would swear I could hear the sound of footsteps walking around, and the moving of chairs. I tell you, sir, it is mighty strange."

"Are you sure that the sounds you heard were not made by the second mate walking on the deck above?"

"No, sir, not at all. He agreed to stay forward on the deck-load till four bells."

"How about the man at the wheel?" said I. "He could walk around on the steering platform and produce such sounds as you heard in the Captain's room."

"Again you are mistaken. The man at the wheel is too scared to make any move but a natural one, such as turning the wheel, and that movement produces no sound down here in fair weather like we are having."

The cook was truly mystified. He was anxious for me to realize the importance of his investigations in the Captain's room, yet with it all he held fast to his materialistic ideals.

"Cook," said I, "you are taking this thing too seriously. I am certain that I have solved this mystery. Riley is certain that it is not Toby, the cat. Now you come along and are ready to prove that the sounds or walking you have observed were not produced by a material power from the deck above."

"I mean," replied he, "that this walking in here was not produced by any action of the second mate or the man at the wheel."

I told him that nevertheless I had the mystery solved, and I would prove it to him. "We have in the lower hold one hundred thousand feet of kiln-dried spruce boards one-half inch thick, and twenty-six to thirty inches wide. They vary in length from eighteen to thirty-six feet. The after bulkhead does not run flush with the deck above, and there are ends of boards that project over and into the runway. With the easy movement of the ship, this will produce a metallic sound that will cause vibration at a distance, and more distinctly under the Captain's room."

At this the cook became very indignant, and told me that my theory was not correct at all.

"Haven't I spent a half hour in the lazarette looking and listening for just such sounds as you describe?"

"Are you sure that there are no rats in his room?"

"If there are, I fail to find them. I have placed cheese around the room to convince myself. On examination of the cheese I couldn't find a tooth mark."

"But why are there no sounds of walking in there now?"

"That is what baffles me," said the cook. "Since we have been talking there has not been a sound from that room."

I sent him to turn in, assuring him that I would sit in the room for an hour or so to see what would happen, and to try to solve a mystery that was beginning to try even my seasoned nerves.

CHAPTER XIII

HIGHER INTELLIGENCE — A VISIT FROM OUT THE SHADOWS

When the steward had gone forward to his bunk, I got a lunch, and was about to sit down by the dining-table to eat it, when I saw the door of the Captain's room open wide.

Then, to my utter amazement, I saw the chair that the dead Captain had sat in for years swing around upon its pivot ready to receive a visitor. I was so startled by the wonderful unseen force that I forgot my lunch and was starting to close the door in the hope of another uncanny experience, when I was halted by a cry from the deck above.

"Hard to starboard, you damned fool. Are you trying to cut her in two amidship?" shouted the second mate.

"Hard over she is," rang out from the man at the wheel.

Instantly I was on deck. The second mate

was over in the lee mizzen-rigging. "What is it, Olsen?" I asked.

"A full-rigged ship away two points on the starboard bow."

To the man at the wheel I said: "Put your helm down and pass to windward of him before you jibe the spanker over, or you will knock Hell out of these old sails." Then to the second mate: "Why do you have to sail all over the ocean to get by that old pea-soup hulk? Don't you see that he has the wind free? Luff her up half a point," I ordered the wheel-man.

We passed so close to windward that we took the wind out of his lower sails. The moon was in the last quarter, and we could see plainly the watch on her deck, and hear the officer swear at the helmsman, saying:

"Keep her off, you damned sheep-herder, or you will cut that mud-scow in two." Then he shouted over to me: "It is the captain of an Irish locomotive you ought to be, you thick-headed pirate, trying to run us down! What's the name of your ship, anyway?"

"Hardship loaded with Poverty," I replied with sarcasm.

As we passed each other the voice of the angry officer grew fainter and fainter, then was lost in the stilly night under Southern skies.

I was amused at the expression of the officer on board of the Yankee clipper, when he spoke of me as the captain of an Irish locomotive. There could be no greater insult to a self-respecting sailorman than this phrase. It means that you would do much better carrying a hod or wheeling a wheelbarrow than handling a ship. I had sailed in those down-east ships and knew their language. They never intend to give one inch on land or sea. Hard luck indeed for the sailor who does not know how to fight, or who shows a yellow streak!

While thus meditating on the cruelties of the old oak ships and thinking what wonderful tales they could tell, my thoughts were suddenly interrupted by a consciousness of fear. Something warm was moving about my feet. On looking down I beheld Toby rubbing his black fur against my feet and legs. . . .

On getting my position of ship at noon today, I noticed the crew tiptoeing around as if they were afraid of disturbing some sleeping baby.

I spoke to Riley, asking what all the hush was about.

"Oh, be the Lord, sir, it is getting turrible on this auld graveyard of a ship. Begorra, we are shure av it now. Auld Charlie seen him prancing up and down the poop deck wid a poipe in his mouth. 'Tis turrible days we be having. The cook said that he proved it himself beyond a question of a doubt that the old bye himself is back on her."

"Well, Riley, I am going to make the Old Man show down tonight. It is put up or shut up for him." Laughing a little at my own fancies, I went aft to the Captain's room, and sat down to watch, to continue to investigate this mystery that was so upsetting the morals of the crew as to endanger their efficiency.

I left the door to the dining-room half open so that the light hung from the center of the ceiling threw its sickly rays into the room. I could hear the man at the wheel make an occasional move with his feet. Then all would be still again. One bell rang,— half-past twelve.

Suddenly the door slammed with a terrible

bang. I knew that there was no draught in the Captain's room to close it in this manner, and I must confess that I was considerably startled. Then I was conscious of some one moving a small stool that stood across from me, over towards the safe at the foot of the bed. I put out my hands to catch the visitor, and not finding anything but air, I reached out and pulled the door open.

To my amazement, the stool had been moved to the safe. I was so unnerved by this that my one thought was to get away, and I went into the dining-room, and unconsciously lit my pipe. When my thoughts sorted themselves it became clear to me that I had been singled out by Destiny to have the privilege of meeting a great and new and unseen Force. If this were so great as to be able to move furniture at will, why, thought I, could it not be harnessed to our material uses? Why could it not be developed to get sails and discharge cargoes? Surely, it would revolutionize the forces of the air and earth, as we know them now.

While these thoughts were taking shape in my

mind, I was brought up with a start by hearing three loud and distinct raps on the door of the Captain's room.

I shook the ashes out of the old corn cob pipe, and entered the room, closing the door behind me. This time I beheld still greater marvels. At the head of the Captain's bed appeared a small light, giving forth no rays, but moving around in the direction of the safe at the foot of the bunk. There it stopped about a minute, then moved over to the desk and gradually disappeared.

"Ah," said I, "you are getting too much for me. Move some more furniture or that safe around this room so that I may alight upon a plan to harness your great power to hand down to future ages."

At that I must have gone to sleep, for I was conscious of nothing more until I heard the cook coming aft with coffee. He was anxious to hear my experience during the middle watch. I told him that there had been no occurrence that was not natural, but that I might have news for him soon.

"Steward," said I, "tomorrow is Christmas

Day. I want you to prepare a good dinner for all hands."

"Oh, yes," he replied, "I have had plum pudding boiling since yesterday. I am going to open a few cans of canned turkey. That, with the cove oyster soup and canned carrots will make a good dinner. I have had a little hard luck with my cake. I forgot to put baking powder in it. But I think that they can get away with it, as there is an abundance of raisins in it."

Christmas morning at half-past twelve found me waiting in the Captain's room listening to rappings on the desk. At times these were loud and then again very weak. I opened the door and turned up the light in the dining-room so that there might be more brightness in the Captain's room. I wanted to see and hear whatever vibrations might be caused from the rappings. As I drew near the writing desk the rapping was centered on the middle drawer. Then it would move to a smaller drawer on the right-hand side and tap very hard. With a shout of joy I sprang to the light at the head of the bed, and lit it.

"At last," I cried, "at last!"

I was satisfied that there were rats in these drawers, and in order that they should not get away I armed myself with a club. I started to pull out the smaller drawer very carefully so that the rodent should not make his escape. To my astonishment I found it locked. I held my ear close to it, but could not hear a sound. Then I proceeded to open the middle drawer with the same caution, but found it open, and nothing in it but a small bunch of keys. My curiosity being aroused, I decided to look for the key on this ring that would open the smaller drawer. After many trials I found one that would fit the lock and on opening it I found, neither the animal, which in spite of my senses' evidence I half expected to see there, nor any other expected alternative, but, most surprising of all, a pair of tiny baby-shoes with a lock of yellow hair, tied with pink ribbon, in each of them.

Back of the shoes was a jewel box, and in it a wedding-ring. Also, wrapped up in paper, was a will made by our late Captain two days before his death. This stated that he had an equity in an apartment house in San Francisco, which he wanted his boys to have. Evidently he had acquired this equity during his last visit to San Francisco. It also stated that there should be no delay in forwarding this will to the above address in West Berkeley, California, U. S. A.

With the discovery of the Captain's treasures, this essence of his personality so revealed, I was carried out of my skepticism for the moment, into feeling his presence beside me, waiting for my word as a friend awaits the voice of a friend. Half unconsciously I spoke aloud: "You have shown me, and I shall obey. You have only to call upon me. Do not be anxious for your ship. I will tell your boys."

"A lonely, lonely Christmas," echoed back vaguely, whether from Beyond or from the storehouse of my imagination, I do not know.

As I replaced his things and started for the deck, the cook's words echoed and re-echoed in my memory, "Does it end here?"

On deck Old Charlie was steering. Looking over the rail at the log, I found that she was cutting the distance to Suva at the rate of nine knots an hour. The breeze was warm, the turquoise sky studded with diamond stars; the three especially bright ones known as the Sailors' Yard were shining in all their splendor.

Away to the south the Southern Cross twinkled and glittered, and was so majestic in its position, that it seemed to command obedience from all other celestial bodies.

CHAPTER XIV

Christmas Day — Our Unwilling Guest the Dolphin

While gazing into the Infinite, analyzing the experience through which I had just passed, and wondering where lay the Land of Shadows, my dreaming was suddenly changed to material things by hearing a terrible fight in the fore part of the ship. Jumping up on the deck-load, and running forward, I could hear Riley shout:

"Club him, you old hen-catcher, you, before he goes through the hawsepipe. That's the way, that's the way. Shure, bad luck to you, you have missed him. Stand back there, stand back there, let me have at him. There he goes again under the lumber. Get me the bar, Pete. Look out, me byes. Shure and be Hivins out he comes again. Strike him between the eyes, Pete. Give me the bar, Pete. Shure'n you couldn't shtrike the sheep barn you was raised in."

"What's all this row about?" I asked.

"Ah, shure, sir, it's me auld friend Neptune would be after sendin' us a Christmas present. He is as fine a bonita as iver greased a mouth, but it's the divil's own toime we have had subduin' him."

"Bring him up on the deck-load and let us look him over."

"Riley," said I, when they had the great fish stretched out before us, "that is a dolphin, and no bonita,— notice the wedge-shaped head, and broad tail. No doubt he was cornered by a school of sword fish, and this fastest fish that swims the ocean had to make a leap for life by jumping aboard our ship. Bring the lantern here, and you will see him change to all colors of the rainbow while he is dying, another proof that he is a dolphin, that is, if he is not already dead."

"Be Hivins, and it's far from dead he is, look at the gills moving." Surely enough, we watched and the beautiful colors came, brilliant blue and green and shaded red, and again I wondered, and it seemed to me that in the passing of the human life there might be just such a color change, invisible to those who are left behind.

Dismissing these thoughts once and for all from my mind, I entered into the long discussion incident to the settlement of claims on the dead dolphin, as to who had discovered him, etc., etc. Broken-Nosed Pete was sure that he had seen him first, very much to the disgust of Riley, who, however, could not deny that his one eye was usually cocked to windward.

I then turned to the men and told them that they need no longer be afraid of the ghost in the Captain's cabin.

Riley spoke up: "And, shure, sir, you wasn't thinking that it was meself that was scared?"

"Why do you carry the belaying-pin aft to the wheel with you, if you are not scared?" said Pete.

"Go wan, you broken-nosed heathen, it's the likes of me that knows the likes av you. You degraded auld beach-comber, haven't I slept in ivery graveyard from Heath Head in Ireland to Sline Head in Galway? Divil a thing did I see only Mugglin's goat."

Riley was about to launch away with Mulligan's goat when I interrupted, reassuring them and telling them that there was no need of carrying belaying-pins to kill the ghost, for it had departed for shores unknown.

"Good luck to it," said Riley, highly pleased, "and more power to it. And shure it is siusible it is to lave on this howly Christmas morning. I remimber one time on an auld side-wheeler running between Dublin and London, it was twelve o'clock —"

Riley's story was cut short by the man at the wheel ringing eight bells, four o'clock. Pete went off to clean the fish, and the others to their watch below, while I turned in, leaving Riley alone with his side-wheeler.

The sentiment of Christmas amongst sailors on the sea makes it a day of strict observances. No work is done outside the working of ship, which is steering or keeping lookout. There is no mat-making, model-making nor patching old clothes in their watch below. They dress in their best clothes, and for those that shave a great deal of time is spent in this operation. No stray bristle has a chance to escape the religious hand of a sailor on a day like this.

It is also a day of letter-writing, with good intentions of forwarding them at the first port, but somehow in the general confusion when in port, they are lost in a whirlpool of excitement. Considering a sign between the ship and the post office reading "Bass' Ale," "Black and White" or "Guinness's Stout," imagine any poor sailor doing his duty to the folks at home! For the moment those glaring and fascinating signs are home to him.

But today is too full of sentiment for him to think of alluring public houses and pretty barmaids. It is given up to religious thoughts with a firm resolution to sin no more.

The spirit of the day had even taken hold of the Socialist cook. In serving dinner I noticed that he had on a clean apron and a white jacket, a great concession for him. I was much attracted by his brogans, which were much too large, and had a fine coating of stove polish to enhance their charm.

"Why have you set a place for the Captain, Steward?" said I.

"Oh, just out of respect for him. You know he wasn't such a bad man after all. Beside, it will make the table look more like a real Christmas dinner. You can just suppose that your invited guest has been delayed, and you can go on with your dinner."

I was beginning to like our cook more and more. It seemed that beneath the hard crust of materialism, there was something very like love and loyalty.

The German noodle soup, the canned turkey, and the plum pudding to top off with was a very befitting dinner at sea. Of course, one must not indulge too freely in plum pudding, especially when its specific gravity exceeds that of heavy metals. This hypothesis was proven to me later in the day.

CHAPTER XV

CRIMP AND SAILOR — THE COOK'S MARXIAN EFFORT

The cook was pleased with my investigation of the Captain's room. "Don't you know," said he, "I was impressed with the unusual sounds there? I was beginning to relinquish my hold on the Material, and to give way more to the unknown and unseen things of life. But you can see that we are all creatures of imagination. There are no limitations to it, especially with those who are superstitious. Now I can plainly understand how such sounds could be produced by rats, just as you say."

He took his stand in the pantry, and continued, from this point of vantage. "It is a shame," he shouted, that there is so much superstition in the world. If there were not so much, the capitalist would not have the opportunity to exploit his ill-gotten goods on the highways and byways of our economic system."

Stirring something in a glass, no doubt extract of lemon, he tipped it to his lips and swallowed it with a grunt of satisfaction.

"With such ignorance in the world," he said, "how are we to combat this scourge of humanity? Let me say here," shaking his fist at me, "the only solution is education without discrimination. With this useful weapon we can equalize the scales of justice. Without it we continue to be slaves to the old and new masters. Take, for instance, the ignorance and superstition of our crew forward. While they are hunting for ghosts the parasites are picking their pockets. What can society expect of them? No wonder they are a prey to apparitions at sea and crimps ashore. Once we were homeward bound from New Zealand to Frisco. The crew, as usual, consisted of many nationalities. She carried twenty-four seamen forward. I frequently talked to these men evenings about joining the Socialist Labor Party, much to the disgust of the Captain. Well, they all agreed that when they should reach San Francisco they would join the organization. I believe that they really intended to, but you know the sailorman ashore scents the rum barrel, and becomes an easy prey to the crimp and boarding-house runner. Two days after our arrival in that wicked city we were paid off by the U. S. Government. I waited until the last man had his money. 'Men,' said I, 'come with me to our hall and join the one organization that is going to redeem the world.'

"The crimp runners were pretty well represented, as they usually are when a ship pays off. They tried every possible means to entice the men away, telling them that they would not have to pay for room or board, and that furthermore they could pick their own ship when they felt like going to sea again. The latter is considered a great concession to a sailor. But the crimps do not stop there. They have old sailors who are kept with them for years, who make it their business to know as many as possible of the men who follow the sea. We had an Irishman in the crew, and this lost the day for me. Just as we started for the hall, out of the crowd strolled a seasoned veteran of the sea. With a shout of joy he fell upon one of our crew, crying:

"'If me eyes don't deceive me, I see Jamey Dugan. Dead or alive, I shake hands with you.'

"Whether Dugan knew the greasy beachcomber or not, I knew that the bunko steering talk would get him. It was very flowery.

"'Why, certainly, you remember me. In Valparaiso. You were in the good old ship so-and-so.'

"I could see that there was no time to lose if I expected to reach the hall with all of them. I mounted a fire-hydrant near by, and pleaded with them, telling them that this crook who had hold of them was nothing but a hireling of the crimp, and tomorrow, all of their money being spent, they would most likely be shipped off to sea in any old tub whose master offered the most money to the boarding-house keeper.

"My pleading was in vain. They kept edging away as if I were a wild beast of the jungle. The influence of the gangster was getting stronger. Again I beseeched and implored these men of the sea to come with me. They only started to move away. It was with a sickened heart that I stepped down from the hydrant. I had no chance with this barnacle of the sea, for they were already starting in his wake for Ryan's saloon across the street."

The cook, lamenting his loss, started to stir up another lemon-de-luxe. Taking advantage of the opportunity, I stole up on deck to relieve the second mate for dinner. He must have thought that I had foundered on the noodle soup and plum-pudding.

The cook and I may not altogether have agreed on the social things of life, but I was with him heart and soul in his fight for better and cleaner conditions for sailors ashore. I, too, know the crimps, and had suffered more than once from their dastardly methods of making money.

They were always on the lookout for anything that resembled a sailor when a ship was ready to sail, and a short-handed captain would offer one of them fifty or a hundred dollars a head blood-money. With that would go from one to two months' advance in wages to the unfortunate victim, which eventually fell into the crimp's hands also. He would not stop even at murder if necessary to fill the required quota.

What if he did ship a dead man or two? They were not supposed to awake for at least twenty-four hours after they were brought aboard. By that time they were under way, and the curses of the captain were lost in sheeting home the upper topsails.

The mate, on the other hand, took a lively interest in restoring the sleeper to life. After he had spent some time clubbing him, and trying every method known to the hard-boiled mates of former times, he would find a belaying-pin, and beat the drugged man on the soles of his shoes. This was the final test. If he did not respond to it, the officer would report to the captain that one of the crew who had just come aboard was dead. Cursing and swearing, the captain would say: "How do you know that he is dead?"

"Well, Captain, I have awakened a great many of them in my time, and there isn't a kick in this fellow."

"Did you try the mirror?"

Holding the mirror at his mouth, to see whether by chance there might be precipitation was the last act. It would never occur to them to feel for the pulse, probably because their hands were too heavily calloused to permit of it. Furthermore, it would never do to lower the mate's dignity in the presence of the crew by so gracious an act.

"No, sir, I have not tried the mirror yet. I am thinking that you have booked a losing."

"Booked Hell," the captain would shout, "Here, take this drink of brandy and pour it into him, then hold the mirror over his mouth. If that doesn't work, throw him overboard."

Those who were shanghaied were not usually sailors. One would find tailors, sheep-herders, waiters and riff-raff of the slums, who had fallen prey to the greed of the boarding-house keeper.

When one did respond to the mate's treatment, he would awake to a living Hell, until the next port was reached, which would take three, four or even five months.

CHAPTER XVI

THE MONTANA COWBOY — A HORSE-MARINE ADVENTURE

There are instances where the Captain and mates of the old time sailing ships have had cause to regret their methods of procuring sailors from the crimps.

When a drugged and shanghaied sailor comes on board the mate looks him over for dangerous weapons.

If he has a sheath knife the mate breaks the point off. If a gun, he takes it aft to the Captain. When the drug-crazed man comes to he is easy to handle. If he should show fight, a crack over the head with a belaying-pin will send him down and out. When the stars disappear and he comes back to earth again, he is very responsive, and willing to scrub decks or anything else that is desired of him.

A Montana cowboy, seeing the sights in a Pacific port, fell a prey to the crimps. Blood money was high. One hundred and fifty dollars was not to be laughed at, when it could be had so easily. The cowboy was given the usual dose of knock-out drops, then thrown into a boat, and rowed off to the ship, which was lying at anchor. When the boat came alongside the ship, the crimp shouted: "Ahoy, Mr. Mate, I have a good sailor for you."

The mate never expected shanghaied men to walk up the gangway. He knew what to expect, and usually gave them the allotted time, about twenty-four hours, to sleep the drug off.

"Are you sure he is a good sailor?" said the mate.

"Oh, yes," replied the crimp, "he is an old-time sailor, we have known him for years. He has been sailing to this port in some of the best ships afloat."

The mate called some members of the crew to get the tackle over the side and yank him aboard. The cowboy was heavy, and he did not yank aboard as easily as some of the other drugged men, very much to the astonishment of the old-time sailors.

They know by the weight on the tackle fall how

to guess what the vocation ashore has been of this latest addition to their number. If the drugged man is a light-weight, he is proclaimed a tailor, if medium weight he is a sheep-herder, and so on.

But they could not find a suitable vocation for this cowboy who was so damned heavy. After long, long pulls, and strong, strong pulls, he landed on deck as limp as a rag. The mate rolled him over with his foot, and seeing that he had no weapons of any kind ordered him thrown on the hatch to sleep it off.

The crimp had relieved him of the cowboy hat, but not the riding shoes, very much to the disgust of the mate, who remarked:

"I have sailed in many ships and with all kinds of sailors, but I will go to Hell if I ever saw a sailor with as long heels on his boots as this fellow has."

Nevertheless he impressed the mate as being a sailor. He had the desert and mountain ruggedness and complexion, and not the sallow dyspeptic look of the tailor, which mates and crew despise so. When the anchor was up, and they were standing out to sea, the mate undertook to awake the cowboy with a force pump.

After the salt water had been played on him about five minutes, he awoke, and realized that he was on board of a ship. He inquired of the mate how he got aboard, and where he was going. The mate answered him very sharply, saying:

"You get up, damn quick, and loose the main-upper-topgallant-sail if you want to get along well and happy in this ship."

He might have been talking the dead languages for all the cowboy knew about upper-topgallant-sails. He rubbed his eyes, and pulling himself together realized that this was not a dream after all, but a stern reality. After looking over the ship and feeling the roll, he eyed the mate with suspicion, saying: "See here, stranger, haven't you made a mistake? Tell me how I came aboard this here ship."

The mate thought the new sailor was having a joke at his expense. Stepping up to him he said, "Damn you, don't you dare to joke with me, or I will break every bone in your body."

"Let me tell you, stranger," said the cowboy,

"I want you to turn this here thing around 'cause I must be a hitting the trail."

This was too much for any good mate to stand, especially when the members of the crew were highly pleased with the new sailor's remark. The mate pulled off his pea-jacket, and tightening his belt, remarked:

"I guess I will teach you how to respect your superiors while you are on board this ship."

The cowboy, seeing that the mate meant business, pulled off his wet coat and vest, also the black silk handkerchief that was tied in a very fashionable knot around his neck and remarked, "Stranger, you be mighty keerful how many bones you break in my body."

Here the mate made a lunge for him, which the boy ducked, and with an upper-cut he sent the mate to the deck in a heap. The mate got up and started for a belaying pin. The crafty range rider was upon him in a second with a left hook to the jaw. The mate went down, and stayed down for some time. Then the second mate, third mate and captain came to the rescue of their first mate. The mates were knocked down as fast as they could get up. The Captain called the crew saying, "Arrest this man and put him in irons for mutiny on the high seas."

This the crew refused to do, because the way this new sailor could use his hands was not at all to their liking, and they were not anxious to take on any rough stuff so early on the voyage.

The Captain, flushed with rage, ran to the cabin shouting:

"I will get my gun and kill this mutineer." The mates picked themselves up and the two went after guns. The cowboy, turning to the sailors, said:

"Here, you critters, get behind a sage bush or something,— get out of range and get out damned quick, for there is going to be Hell shot out of this here ship in about a minute." Reaching down in his riding boots he pulled out two forty-fives and backed over to the starboard bulwarks to await the signal from the cabin.

He did not have to wait long. The Captain came roaring up the companionway, thinking that the new sailor at the sight of the gun would run and get under cover. But not so with this one, far from it. There he stood, a plain and visible target for the Captain's and mate's guns.

While the Captain was running along the lee alleyway of the bridge-deck, the cowboy called to him, saying:

"Can you kill from the hip, Mister? If you can't you'd better get close and shoot straight."

The Captain was too angry to utter a sound. It was bad enough to knock his three mates down and out, without heaping insult upon insult by asking if he could shoot straight. The blow he had got on the jaw from this untamed sailor he considered enough to justify him in killing on sight anyway, for it would be days before he could bring his jaws together on anything harder than pea soup or bread pudding.

With these maddening thoughts twitching his nautical brow, he swung from the bridge-deck onto the main deck. There in front of him stood the new mariner leaning against the bulwarks with his hands behind his back. The Captain's gun was swinging at arm's length in the right hand, but not pointed toward the cowboy.

This code of ethics pleased the cowboy, for he remarked to the Captain: "Remember you draw first, and if you have any message for the folks at home now is the time to send it."

Hearing the mates coming, the Captain took courage, and raised his gun as if to shoot, when a shot rang out and his right arm fell limply to his side. With a spring of a wild animal the cowboy changed for a new position. He jumped onto the main hatch, where he could command a view of the ship fore and aft. No sooner had he changed to his new position, than the mates appeared on the main deck and ordered him in the King's name to surrender or take the consequences.

"I don't know anything about your kings," remarked the cowboy, "but I do know I'm going back to my ole horse and I'm going mighty quick. Let me tell you, strangers, I want you to turn this here ship back. I'll give you five minutes to make up your minds."

The Captain broke the silence by ordering the ship back to port, saying, to save his dignity, that he could never go to sea wounded as he was, and was also anxious to bring this sailor to the bar of justice for mutiny and attempted murder on the high seas.

"Before you obey the orders of your boss here," said the cowboy, addressing the crew, "I want your guns. You know it is dangerous for children like you to be handling something you don't know much about."

Evidently the Captain was in great pain, for he commanded the mates to give up their weapons, which they did very reluctantly after the ship had tacked and stood in for port again. To make matters worse, the cowboy walked the weather side of the bridge-deck, and practically commanded the ship until she dropped anchor.

Then the police boat came off and took captain, mates and cowboy ashore to the hall of justice, where the new sailor put a kink in the crimp, sending him for five years to the penitentiary for drugging and shanghaing him. He also caused the Captain and first mate to exchange their comfortable quarters aboard ship for uneasy cells in jail; six months for the mate and a year for the Captain. . . .

The old Hell Ships have passed away into the murky horizon, to be seen no more, and with them have gone the old sailors, some to the Land of Shadow, others to pass their remaining years working ashore, and many to that most coveted place on earth, Snug Harbor. A new age has dawned upon the mariner of today. He sails on ocean greyhounds, where there are no yards to square, no topsails, no tiller ropes to steer with. He doesn't have to sail four years before the mast to learn how to become a sailor. Steam, the simplified, has made it pleasant and easy for him. He no longer requires the tin plate and hook pot, nor has he any place for the donkey's breakfast. (The latter used to be supplied by the crimp and consisted of a handful of straw tucked into a cheap bed tick; that was the sailor's bed in the old days.)

Today he is supplied with everything necessary for his comfort, even to five hundred cubic feet of air space, and food as good as he was likely to get ashore.

The cracker or hardtack hash was an art years ago, and required the skill of a French chef. It is even possible that the French chef would not have scorned what the old sailor discarded in making this sumptuous repast. The first process of this delicious dish was to economize for days to save enough hardtack. Secondly, it was necessary for it to soak at least forty-eight hours.

By that time you were sure that all living creatures had forsaken their pleasant abode for a breath of fresh air or a swim around the hook pot.

When you were satisfied that the hardtack was malleable, you would mix in what salt horse you could spare without stinting yourself too much, and anything else that happened to be around. Then came the supreme task, getting a concession from the cook to bake it. It required much study as to how to approach the "Doctor," for this was his title in important functions. Should he be so generous with you as to grant an interview for this noble concession, you were to be complimented, and considered in line for promotion to the black pan. It is only a brother in death that could share the remnants from the Captain's table. Hence the black pan.

The sailor of today no longer need covet the crumbs from the captain's table, he is fed à la carte and waited on by uniformed waiters; even his salary is more than captains received twenty to thirty years ago in sailing ships.

CHAPTER XVII

THE FRAGRANT SMELL OF THE ALLURING PALMS

Away to the westward the sun was sinking into the deep, with small fleecy clouds guarding the last bright quivering rays as if giving a signal to make ready for the lovely night. So Christmas had come and departed with the setting of the sun.

I was thinking of him who had also departed so suddenly to the land of eternal rays, and wondered if the great Nazarene should not have said, " Peace to those who have passed away, and good will to those whom they have left behind."

For the next ten days the wind held steady, and one could see from the restlessness of the crew, particularly Dago Joe, that we were nearing land. I had sent a man aloft to see if he could pick up Wallingallala Light. I was sure that if our chronometer was right we should pick it up about two o'clock in the morning. I decided to sail through Namuka Passage, thereby cutting off the distance to Suva about three hundred and fifty miles. Otherwise it would be necessary to sail to the southward of the Archipelago, and the danger of the latter course was the southeast trades, which usually die out twenty degrees south of the Equator.

As Suva lay 18° 22', I was sure I could hold the wind through the Passage, if I could keep away from the uncharted coral reefs which are so dangerous to navigation among those islands. At half-past three in the morning Broken-Nosed Pete sang out from the foretop, "A light on the port bow." I took the binoculars and ran up the mizzen-rigging. There was the long-looked-for light.

I changed the course after getting bearings on the light, and headed her for Namuka Passage. After entering the Passage it was necessary to change our course from time to time, and this had to be done by log and chart, in order to avoid the projecting reefs which jutted out from the island. Many of these reefs extend from three to five miles from each island. The navigator never loses his position of ship, and great care must be taken in making allowances for currents.

About six o'clock we were well into the Passage and abreast of Boscowen Island, better known as Cap Island. Away to the southwest lay Vite Vuva, which was the island we were bound for. The wind was freshening, and when passing an island great gusts of wind would swoop on us, which made it necessary to take in our staysails.

The fragrant smell of the alluring palms was beginning to fascinate the crew, with the exception of Riley, who wore a rather troubled look. When I asked him if he was sick he replied in the negative, "Sick would you have me? Shur'n the divil a bit is it sick I am. Auld Charlie has been telling me it's cannibals there are on these islands, but shure I don't belave a wurd that old wharf rat says."

"Well, Riley," said I, "Charlie may be right. No doubt somewhere in these islands there may lurk a few sturdy savages who wouldn't hesitate a moment to recommend that a man like you be cooked and served table d'hôte at one of their moonlight festivals. They much prefer the white meat to the dark, and you will admit there are some choice pieces in you."

"There are, me bye, but I'll be keeping meself intact and the divil a man-eater will iver lay a tooth in me, if Michael Dennis Riley knows anything."

"Stay close to the ship," said I, "and don't wander too far afield and I doubt if there is much danger, as long as you keep sober and have your eye peeled to windward."

"Be Hiven, sor, and that is what I will be doing. As for keeping sober, shure and that is aisy for me. It is only on rare occasions that I ever take a drop of the crayture. Begorra, and it's the pledge I'll be taking while I'm amongst these heathen."

The speed we were making did not encourage me in the least. We were logging eleven knots, and if she kept this up we would be off Suva Harbor about two-thirty in the morning; then it would be necessary to lie off Suva till the pilot came aboard some time during the forenoon. The chart showed it was about seven miles from the entrance of the channel between the coral reefs to the harbor. As there were no tug-boats here, I figured that by the time the pilot rowed off to where I should be in the offing, it would indeed be late in the morning. But I was much worried at having to spend a night dodging these dangerous reefs which were not even marked by a bell-buoy.

Towards evening, while passing between two islands, the wind fell very light. The channel was narrow, and it looked for a time as if we were in danger of drifting onto the south reef of Vite Vuva Island. What little breeze there was carried to our ears the enchanting voices of the natives singing their island songs. The cook was coaxing Toby to indulge in age-old brisket, but without success, and turning to me he said, "What a pity it is that our world isn't full of song and laughter like that of these happy natives. Their day of toil is over, and with it comes the song of happiness. There are no landlords here to dispossess you, no licensed thugs hired by crooked corporations to club you while you are working for the interest of the downtrodden. I tell you that some day the world will be just such a place to live in as these isles, no worries, no troubles and damned little work."

CHAPTER XVIII

Suva Harbor — The Reef and the Lighthouses

As we nosed by the reef, and got the island on our beam, the wind came to our rescue, and with staysails set I laid a course for Suva Harbor. At one o'clock we picked up Suva lights, the two lighthouses which marked the entrance to the harbor. One light is about on sea level, the other has an altitude of some two hundred feet, being back and up the hill and in direct line with the first. When these two lights bear due north you have the channel course into Suva Harbor.

When I had these lights in range I decided to run in and take a chance, rather than stay out and wait for the pilot. Another reason why I was anxious to get in was that the barometer was falling and it looked like rain. This being the hurricane season, I was not at all pleased with the mackerel skies of the early morning. The channel is very narrow between the reefs, and great care must be taken in steering one's course.

After jibing her over and pointing her into the channel, I had Broken-Nosed Pete take the wheel, with instructions that if he got off the course his neck would be twisted at right angles to his nose. Pete was a good helmsman, and could be trusted in close quarters like those we were about to sail through.

Until we passed into the harbor my interest in the schooner "Wampa" could be had for a song. With waves breaking on either side of us as we were passing through, and expecting every moment to strike the reef, moments seemed like centuries, and not to me alone. The only sound that came from the crew was from Riley, and he did not intend it for my ears.

The noise of the breakers to windward was not so bad for Riley and his one eye, but to have it repeated on his blind side was asking too much of an honest sailor. He shouted to Old Charlie, "Glory be to God, Charlie, and it's drowned we will be in sight of land. In the name of the Father, what made him attempt it on a night like this? Look, look, Holy Saint Patrick, look at the breakers. Ah, and it's high and dry we'll be. Bad luck to the day I ever set foot on this auld barge! She isn't fit for a dog to sail in."

The harbor end of the reef was marked by a light on a small cutter, which was so dim that one would almost have to have a light to find it. After rounding this insignificant light we had deep water and a large harbor.

Just as day was breaking we dropped anchor, after an eventful voyage of fifty-four days from Puget Sound. At eight o'clock an East Indian doctor came on board, and lining the crew up for inspection, required every man to put out his tongue. From the looks of the above-mentioned he seemed pleased with the health of the crew. He left, after looking over the official log book to make sure that the Captain had not been murdered.

The customs men followed him aboard, and being assured that we were not pirates, departed to where the brandy and soda offered a more tempting interest. As I expected, the pilot came alongside about nine-thirty, very much disgusted to think that I should dare to run the channel without the guidance of his steady head and hand.

Had he not been here for fifteen years doing this work which required skill and courage, piloting ships of all nations into and out of this dangerous channel? What was it to him (with a clinking glass), whether the conversation took the shape of the battle of Balaclava or the bombardment of Alexandria? Let the ships lay in the offing and await his pleasure. They were helpless without him, and must await his guidance to reach safe anchorage.

He scrambled over the side, and adjusting his monocle to look me over, said in an accent that would make a cockney cab-driver take to honest toil, "Ahem, ahem, where is your captain?"

"He is somewhere around the Equator in 145° west longitude," I said. "Ow, ow, I see. He abandoned the ship, I suppose."

"Yes," said I, "he left much against his will. It is rather strange, is it not?"

"Well, I'll be blowed to think he should have departed in this manner."

Riley, who was coiling down the main boom tackle fall, was more interested in the English pilot than in coiling ropes. The last remark of the pilot re-echoed back from him in words not befitting this high command.

"Shur'n it's more av them that ought to be laying at the bottom of the sea with a mill stone around their neck."

The way Riley's one eye would alternate from the pilot to the little town across the harbor, and the way his lips twitched suggested to me what was going on in his mind. To think he had sailed seventy-five hundred miles to find a specimen like this! "To hell with the pledge and Cannibal Isles, isn't the sight of this enough to drive any poor Irishman into swearing allegiance to John Barleycorn for the rest of his life?"

CHAPTER XIX

Introducing Captain Kane, Mrs. Fagan and Mrs. Fagan's Bar

After convincing the pilot of the Captain's death, I was given a severe reprimand for coming into the harbor alone. When he went ashore I had the small boat lowered, and, putting on a pair of the dead Captain's shoes, also his shirt and pants, I had Broken-Nosed Pete row me to the landing place on the wharf.

I wanted to look up the consignee and see where he wanted the cargo of lumber. There were a few cutters anchored in the harbor, but no ships. As we neared the wharf, I noticed a neat and clean little steam cutter lying along the south side of the wharf, and judged from the three-pound gun on her deck that she was a revenue cutter. On the wharf stood many natives, male and female. I was particularly attracted to the native men, who were wonderful types of physical development, standing six feet or more, with broad shoulders and deep chests. The muscles ran smoothly in their arms and legs, and their tapering thighs and agile feet made a picture seldom seen in the northern latitudes. They had no worries and troubles in dealing with the tailors and dressmakers. Adam and Eve fashions still prevailed here, although some of the more prominent wore a yard or two of white linen instead of the fig leaves. This, contrasted with the shiny dark skin and the white-washed hair, which had a vertical pitch, rather distinguished them in appearance from their more humble brethren.

Broken-Nosed Pete was so fascinated by "the female of the species," that he forgot to moor the boat. As the latter was drifting away from the wharf I gave him instructions to be more prudent,— to make fast the boat, and remain there until my return. Evidently Pete was not looking for this rebuke, for he answered in a voice that could be heard the width of the harbor saying, "Aye, aye, there seems to be a hellish current, sir."

As I started to walk up the wharf I was met

by a young man wearing a Palm Beach suit. "You are the Captain of the 'Wampa,' I believe," said he, "I represent Smith & Company here, and your cargo is consigned to us." After showing me where the lumber was to go, he told me that I would have to raft it ashore. This was rather discouraging to me, as the distance was about one mile from the ship and I had never had any experience with work of this kind, but on account of shallow water at the dock I had no other alternative and decided to raft the cargo ashore as he directed.

He invited me to his office, telling me that he believed there was mail there for the ship. In passing a hotel at the end of the wharf he suggested a highball, which was served in due course by a red-headed Irish barmaid. I was then introduced to a number of Hibernians, noticeable among whom was a very fat and blubbery looking creature with an unusually large nose. His black beard was streaked with gray, his mouth had a sort of an angular twist, and in opening it one could see a few stray tusks, so solitary that it seemed they must be quite conscious of the old surroundings. The shirt, with its nicotine and other stains, was open at the neck, displaying a black and long-haired breast. This he seemed to be very proud of.

After telling me that his name was Captain Kane, and that he was the Captain of the "Pongon," the revenue cutter which I had noticed lying alongside the wharf, he put his hand to his breast and began to twist the black hair. This was probably an act of official dignity as Captain of the "Pongon," and representative of the British Government in the Fiji Archipelago. I got the mail, which consisted of three letters, one for the cook, and one for me from the owners, instructing me to proceed home in ballast to San Francisco. The other was addressed to Nelson, the Dane. When I got back aboard the ship it was noon, and raining as it knows how to rain in this country. It was not dropping down, but a continuous stream as if running through a sprinkler.

The afternoon was given to taking off deck-lashings and getting a line ashore in order to be able to pull the raft to the wharf. This operation used up almost all the rope on the ship.

About seven o'clock the crew came aft to say

that they were going ashore and wanted some money to spend. Oh, no, not at all for whiskey, just a few necessary things such as socks, tobacco and handkerchiefs. (Whoever heard of a sailor buying a handkerchief while the ready oakum is to be had for the asking!) I assured them that tomorrow I would draw on the owners, and give them one pound each to spend on these luxuries. They went forward growling and grumbling, and not at all pleased with this proposition. I believe that Broken-Nosed Pete's description of what he had seen at the wharf weighed heavy on their minds.

In the morning we started the raft by taking four long two-by-sixes and lashing them at the ends, thus forming a square, then launching it over the side, and making it fast to the ship. We started to stow the lumber on the ship, running the boards fore and aft, then athwart ships. After having stowed a few tiers, the raft took shape, but great care had to be taken in starting it, as it was hard to keep the first boards from floating away. The raft could not draw over six feet, otherwise we could not float it ashore, but with this draft we could raft twenty thousand feet ashore and escape the shallow places in the harbor.

I went ashore towards noon to hire ten natives to help unload cargo. Much to my surprise, the native Fijian is a man of leisure and not of toil. Shell-fishing is good, and the yams and bananas are within easy reach, so this gentleman prefers to bask in the sunshine rather than to work for a paltry shilling.

I was about to go to the office of Smith & Company to see what they could do for me about getting help, when I espied Captain Kane strolling up the wharf. From the way his legs were spread apart one could see that his cargo was something different from lumber. As he approached me I noticed the cigar was so short that it was singeing his black beard and mustache. He greeted me warmly, saying, "How's she heading, sonny?" and insisted that I join him in a glass, as he usually took one about this time of day.

On the way to the hotel I told him how hard it was going to be for me to get help. He stopped suddenly, and, turning around to look at the harbor as if to make sure that there were no blockade runners in the offing, he fanned himself with his cheese-cutter cap, then turned towards me saying, "Why, man alive, I can load your ship down with coolies. Do you see those," pointing to a couple of small men, "they are our workers here. They come in from the Solomon group. I will get you as many as you want for two shillings a day and meals. As for these natives, they are damned lazy scoundrels, that's what they are, they won't work at all if they can help it."

Mrs. Fagan greeted us with a smile, asking us in the good old Irish way what our pleasure might be. Her red hair was much in need of combing and lacked the delicate wave of the tonsorial artist. We were joined by the pilot, who was on his way to give his boat's crew a little excursion around the harbor. "One must keep them in practice, you know. Goodness knows when a coolie ship may heave in sight, and I must be there to guide her in. Oh, yes, I must do my duty rain or shine."

CHAPTER XX

Reminiscences of Old Clipper Days

One could see from the yawn and grunt that Captain Kane gave, that if the pilot went on talking he would disregard all rules of the road and make it a head-on collision. How could he respect this thing, that called itself captain and pilot, when all he commanded was an open boat with a few black oarsmen; "It is practice you want," said Captain Kane, raising his glass and draining the last dregs from Mrs. Fagan's highball, setting the glass down on the bar with a bang that seemed to further derange Mrs. Fagan's red hair.

She turned around exclaiming, " May the Lord save us and phat was that?"

"Let me tell you," said Captain Kane to the pilot, wiping his mouth, " that I don't think you know Hell about doing your duty. Here's a man " — patting me on the shoulder — " that squared away and ran the reef while you were asleep, yes, damn you, asleep. You talk about duty!" The little wisp of hair on Captain Kane's head no longer lay in quiet repose, but started to ascend as if controlled by the angular motions of his hands and feet. The illuminating light in his bleary eyes continued, and he said in a voice that sounded like the rolling surf, "Fifty years ago, running between Ceylon and the United Kingdom, in the old tea clippers where our topsails and top-gallant sheets were locked with a padlock, and where we got a bonus from the owners whenever we carried away a sail. Those were the days!"

He brought his clubbed fist down on the bar with such force that he jarred many of the glasses that were arranged around the beer pump handles. Mrs. Fagan whispered to me that the Captain was not himself today at all, at all, that he seldom gave way like this. "You talk about duty to me," Captain Kane continued, "but I've seen the time when every damned man of us were tied to the rigging during a typhoon. Never a reef nor a furled sail, while the Captain held the padlock keys. Oh, boys, those were the days, and you come around here talking to me about your duty. Go on with you now before I forget that I am Captain of His Majesty's ship 'Pongon.'"

The pilot was much distressed by this outburst of anger from Captain Kane. As he adjusted his monocle with trembling fingers before replying, a side door opened and Mr. Tim Fagan, proprietor of the Pier Hotel, greeted us with a grin, saying, " 'Tis a foine day we be havin', men, and how are you all this morning?"

The contrast between Mr. and Mrs. Fagan was interesting, and one could see that the eugenic situation had not yet reached south of twenty-three.

His costume was that which is worn by the English lodge gate-keeper. He stood about five feet four, in the long stockings and the knee pants, the spiral legs, the number ten boots. This rig was coupled with the fringe of a beard extending from ear to ear, partly displaying a small chin and upper lip. Such an upper lip is seldom seen outside South Africa, but with him it had assumed such vast proportions that there was little to see of the face. The wart or button that was intended for a nose was pushed up the face and in line with the gray eyes. The mouth was in contrast to the upper lip, but its expansion was lost in the sandy stubble of the side whiskers.

Mrs. Fagan looked adoringly at her beloved spouse and said, "Tim, it's yourself that will treat the gintlemen."

It was with great difficulty that Captain Kane reached a small shack made of bamboo poles and palm leaves. On entering we were confronted with a sight long to be remembered, for there, sitting around in a circle were fourteen natives of the Solomon Islands chewing kara root, which, after much masticating, they spit into a large earthen-ware dish. The kara root when properly masticated is then collected, put through a sort of churning process and made into a drink which is known as Fiji grog. It resembles oatmeal water, which is a familiar drink among our northern harvest hands, but lacks its obvious peculiarities. The natives greeted the Captain with a salaam-san and proffered him a cup of the thick and slimy substance. The Captain refused, saying that it was near his lunch hour and he preferred not to indulge on an empty stomach, which I was pleased to see, for if he had taken aboard some of this mysterious looking cargo and mixed it in his watertight compartment there would have been a vacant chair at lunch on board His Majesty's ship " Pongon."

CHAPTER XXI

Unloading Cargo — Again the Master — Native Police

I had no difficulty in hiring ten of the little men, and took them off to the ship to work cargo. In the afternoon we hauled a raft of lumber ashore. I was greatly encouraged with this process of unloading; of course it lacked the noise of the steam winch and the occasional profanity of the Frisco longshoremen, but this was the South Sea Isles where work was a pleasure.

I drew thirty pounds (a hundred and fifty dollars), remembering that the crew had some "purchases" to make that evening. After supper they came aft, dressed in their best clothes, and repeated their demands of the evening before.

After giving each member of the crew forward one pound, and the second mate and cook two pounds, they got in the boat and pulled ashore, leaving me and Toby, the black cat, to guard the ship. I remained long after sunset on deck listening to the natives singing and playing their guitars. The sound, mingled with the noise of the surf breaking on the reefs beyond the purring of Toby, created a lullaby that would soothe the wildest intellect.

Leaving Toby on deck to play with the cockroaches, I went aft to the cabin to make the report of the day. While thus working I was interrupted by a strange noise in the Captain's room. I thought it was Toby going his rounds, but upon investigation I found that he was on deck and sitting by the galley door. I was busy with an example in proportion. If it took one day to unload twenty thousand feet of lumber how many days would it take to unload five hundred thousand? I seated myself at the table again, but was brought up with a sudden start on hearing three loud and distinct knocks on the dead Captain's door. I found myself saying, "Yes, Captain, I will attend to it at once."

In my excitement of the past few days I had forgotten to mail the dead Captain's last will to Berkeley, California. I jumped up and opened the door leading to his room. Lighting the light and going to a small drawer in the desk, I took out the will, also the little shoes, and the pink ribbons, and yellow curls, and started ashore to mail them to the above address in the U. S. A. I did not stop now to write the letter, which I knew must also go, and which would be so very hard for me to write.

I made the small boat fast at the landing, and hurried to where I could get stamps, for I was bound that these packages should leave on the next north-bound steamer.

As I neared the Pier Hotel I was surprised to see Riley standing outside the door talking in a loud and profane voice. In passing him I could hear him say, "Ah go-wan, you dirty Connemara crook, shur'n I knew your father, he used to eat swill out of the swill barrels."

With this a chair came bouncing through the door, which increased my speed for the Post Office. Evidently, Mr. Fagan and Riley had been having some political argument, for in the distance he was shouting, "Parnell was a gintleman and a scholar!"

Riley's shouting was evidently disturbing the peace of the harbor, for a great many of the natives, men and women, were running towards the Pier Hotel where he was holding forth.

As I walked to the more thickly settled part of the town I stopped and asked a white man where the Post Office was. On being told it was down by the Club Hotel, the anxiety to relieve my mind of this obligation caused me to put on more speed, and I shoveled along in the Captain's heavy and much too large boots. Arriving at the Club Hotel I was informed that the Post Office was closed. The genial host, a thick heavy-set Australian, supplied me with stamps, paper and envelopes, and I wrote to the owners telling them of the Captain's death, and sent the package in their care, with instructions to forward it to the proper address.

I felt greatly relieved of my responsibility to the Captain and owners when the host assured me that he would take care of the postage in the morning. Becoming suddenly conscious of the real picturesqueness of these islands and anxious to see the natives at closer range, I called up all the old beach combers in the hotel to have a drink. This seemed to please the proprietor, for he shouted, "Come on, men, breast the bar!"

I noticed Broken-Nosed Pete in the corner having a very confidential chat with a villainous-looking man. They were so occupied that they failed to hear the cheery command of the proprietor. The attractive barmaid was very much annoyed at my ordering ginger ale, turning around and looking at herself in the glass and adjusting her white crocheted cap as if to make sure that she was really awake and not dreaming. " Whoever heard of a sailor drinking ginger ale," she might have said, " haven't they come here from the four corners of the earth always thirsty for the rum that makes them merry and gay? Besides, you can never loosen up a man on ginger ale."

His spendings in the rum shops in this case are not at all to the liking of the pretty barmaids, who flatter themselves that they get the last penny from the sailor just off the sea. I was reminded of the time by seeing an old-fashioned clock hanging to the right of the bar, when suddenly a trap door on top of the old clock opened, and a cuckoo hopped out cooing the hour of eleven o'clock. So absorbed had I been in meeting with the old shell-backs, who were lined along the bar at my expense drinking Old Tom and soda that I became oblivious both of the flight of time and the slow trickling away of my money. I made a hasty getaway for the open.

Outside the night was warm and everything peaceful and tranquil. The rolling hills to the eastward were illuminated by the silvery rays of a rising moon. The occasional hum of the disgusted mosquito who had missed his mark was all that seemed to disturb the peace of this quaint Fijian town. The moon took flight, squeezing and pushing her way through the far-off stately palms. As she began to throw ghostly shadows from the native house tops, I felt the fascination of these islands as never before. The soft trade winds, the silvery rippling waters, the lullaby from the reef beyond, the cooing and gurgling of the surf as it played upon the coral beech below, were enchanting.

The distant call of the native boatman shoving off with his cargo of vegetables and fruits for early market, caused silvery threads of sound in the night, and a parrakeet chattered as he gave way to a more worthy rival. The tune of the sea-gull reached me as he dove from on high and missed his wiggling fish.

While listening to these strange and interesting sounds, I was rudely interrupted by boisterous laughter coming from the direction of the Pier Hotel. I thought of Riley, and hastened there, thinking that his political argument must have taken a serious trend.

Much to my surprise Riley was not to be seen, but there stood the Socialist cook, perched high on a dry goods box with a large mug of ale in one hand and a black cigar in the other. There were a few native men and women standing around, evidently much amused by the cook's gestures. Back of him, beside a sickly and yellow oil lamp, stood two natives dressed in loose tunics, whose sleeves were cut off at the elbow. They also wore short skirts coming down to the knee, and below that was nature's own. What attracted me most was the coloring of this strange uniform.

As I edged closer I noticed that this kilty-look-costume was a very dark blue, but the trimmings were getting on my nerves. The wearers were standing with one side to the oil lamp, and from this angle I could see that the dresses were trimmed with red borders about three inches wide above the neck. The cut-off sleeves also had their share of this Satanic display. The short petticoat was more conspicuous. This, contrasted with large feet and yellow legs, showing the blood-red border on the indigo skirt, was a coloring seldom seen in any man's country.

As they whispered to each other I noticed that they had long clubs belted onto their hands. The cook, between a puff on the black cigar and a drink of Bass' Famous was decrying the British government for making slaves of them. After much persuasion I took the cook in tow for the ship. I did not like the look of His Majesty's Fijian policeman, especially since I was so much dependent on early breakfasts for both the crew and natives.

At the row-boat the cook hesitated, saying: "Just one more before we part." When I answered him in the negative he straightened up and squared his shoulders, saying: "To Hell with monarchies; I shall give them the ballot to do with as they may." The ginger ale in this instance was more powerful than the famous Bass' ale and I shouldered the cook easily up the gangway. I noticed as I did so that the cat-boat was not alongside. Evidently the crew was still enjoying Fiji hospitality. This was proven on reaching the deck, for the only sound that greeted us was Toby purring and wagging his black tail, happy in the knowledge that even a drunken cook was preferable to the lonely swinging anchor light on the fore-stay.

I left the cook, after assuring him that I would lend my assistance in starting a socialist colony on one of these islands. From the way he tumbled into the bunk there would be little time consumed in making his toilet in the morning. Perhaps it was just as well if one denies the claims of bedbugs, cockroaches and mosquitoes. They had waited patiently for the past six hours for just this event. What a wonderful opportunity they would find in this fat and blubbery creature lying there in an ecstasy of bliss, with not a groan to disturb their peaceful recreation. Only a matter of a slight incision on a choice part, then insert the valve and turn on the centrifugal pump and all would be done to their great satisfaction. But this slumbering animal was now done up in impenetrable strata of clothes, which ruined their sport.

Removing the hat and loosing the black and red tie from around his neck, I blew out the light, and left him to determine a battle for the survival of the fittest.

CHAPTER XXII

Shore Leave — The Web-Toed Sailor — The Missionary Ship

I was wondering whether to go ashore to look for the crew, when I heard the second mate's voice saying: "Easy on your port oars. Give away hard on your starboard." As they came alongside the gangway I could see Riley and the Russian-Finn asleep in the bow of the cat-boat. Dago Joe was missing, and the others had had about all the rum they could stand. I gave the second mate orders to leave Riley and the Russian-Finn in the boat, as it was dangerous to try to get them on board while they were so drunk. Swanson spoke up, saying: "To Hell with you, we do what we damned please."

I was rather upset by this remark coming from the big Swede. I should have thought that he would have had enough of fighting on the trip south. Evidently the booze was working on him and he was intending revenge. I stepped over to the pin-rail and pulled out a wooden belaying-pin. Booze or no booze, I was going to make this brute respect me if I had to resort to old-time methods. Running down the gangway, I ordered all that could walk up to get there damned quick and pointed to Swanson, saying: "You will be the first to leave the boat." As the ship swung with the outgoing current, the moon revealed the expression of hatred on Swanson's face. The high cheek bones, the knitted viking-brows, the large cruel mouth, showing the irregular and vicious-looking tusks, the eyes no longer blue, whose pupils were so enlarged that the color had disappeared,— all this gave him just the look of a wild animal at bay.

Swanson jumped from the stern-sheets to the center of the boat, shouting: "Shove her off and we will go ashore again, and you may go to Hell." As he reached for the boat hook to shove her off or to use it on me if it should come handy, I did not wait for him to decide. Jumping into the boat, I knocked him down and ordered the others aboard.

Whether my sudden irruption amongst them with the belaying-pin was a counter-irritant for the booze they had within them or not I don't know. But the boat was cleared in two minutes, leaving Swanson, Riley and the Finn lying in the bottom. The second mate, although trying with a thick tongue to proclaim his innocence of having had even a glass of ale, was making heavy weather of it while going up the gangway. I reached for the water dipper and poured the salt, but warm, sea water over Swanson. After a few applications of this stimulating treatment he arose to his feet saying, " I tank I go on board now." I followed him up the gangway and forward to his bunk to make sure there would be no tricking from this brute. I remembered the cowardly kick on my forehead and resolved if there was any kicking to be done I would do it.

Walking aft, I heard splashing as if some one was overboard. On reaching the gangway I discovered that the Finn was missing from the boat. Ahead of the cat-boat lay a raft of lumber, and on the outside of it I could plainly see bubbles coming up, and wondered if this could not be the action of a vegetable gas.

But to my horror the Russian's head popped out of the water, and with it came a blood-curdling scream as he writhed about in his death struggles. Instead of making for the raft, he was fanning and kicking the water away from it.

I dropped the belaying-pin, and, slashing the shoe strings of the Captain's boots, jumped out of them and overboard after the drowning Finn. As I swam near him his hands went up and with a shriek he sank below. After several attempts at diving, I finally caught him by the arm, and arose to the surface. Swimming over to the gangway, I caught hold of the boat painter, and, throwing his arms over the rope, I managed to crawl onto the lower platform, then pulling and struggling with this dead burden, I gradually made my way to the deck.

I dumped him down on the break of the poop and ran for the cook's pork barrel. It wasn't that I was so terribly interested in this lifeless thing, but I was interested in knowing that should I lose him I would be forced to sail short-handed, as there were no sailors here who cared to stray far away from the cocoanuts and yams.

When it came to rolling I gave him the benefit of the doubt. I rolled him under the barrel and over it, and stimulated him with artificial respiration. After about one hour he began to show signs of life. I then carried him forward to his bunk, taking off his shoes and stockings.

My attention was caught by his feet, for he had one large toe on each foot, and in place of the smaller toes all that remained was a thin tissue or web, extending from the large toe to where the smaller one should be. Then it dawned upon me that the reason this man never went barefooted was his bashfulness of these duck-like feet. After covering him over in the bunk, I hurried to where Riley was lying in the boat, finding him cuddled up with his head between his legs.

I decided to leave him there, but secured him fast with a rope, in such a way that when he became sober it would be necessary for some one to come to his rescue; I was not going to take any chances on having to be the pearl diver to fish Riley from the depth of Suva Harbor.

Away to the eastward the faint rays of a new day were shown in an amber sky streaked with brilliant pink. Taking the cook's alarm clock, I went below to secure some sleep before five o'clock. While fixing the mosquito net over the port hole in my room I was startled by hearing a cry which resolved itself into, " Murder, murder, begorra it's tied they have me. Hivenly Father, to think I should be ate up by those damned cannibals and not a soul in sight to see the last of Michael Dennis Riley."

I would gladly have left Riley tugging and pulling at the diamond hitch that bound him, but I was afraid that his cries of murder would attract the Fiji policemen ashore. It required tact and skill and diplomacy to untie Riley. He was snapping and kicking, and dangerous to get near. He was calling on all the angels in Heaven to witness the terrible crime he was about to be subjected to. I assured him that his old tough and tarry hide was not even fit for a shark to eat, let alone a decent Fiji cannibal.

He seemed to scent a kindly influence, but was rather inclined to resent the idea of having a tarry hide. After his hands and feet were free he wanted to fight it out there, and then saying that it did not matter a tinker's damn who called him this name, but there was no man that could get away with an insulting remark like calling him a tarry-hide or an old shell-back.

"Be Hivins, the cannibals are bad enough," he said, "but to call a dacent man a name like this is too much for the pride of Ireland to stand."

As he struggled to his feet I stepped over to the blind side of him and tightened the clove hitch around his neck. I had no desire to let this drunk-crazed Irishman loose on the boat. After much coaxing and reassuring he finally recognized me and offered an apology. I took the hitch off his neck, and let him up to the deck, where he begged for one more hour's sleep. I called the cook to get breakfast, as it was nearly five o'clock, and had a look at the Finn, who seemed none the worse for his plunge in the harbor. The freaky and webby toes were sticking out over the bunk and I wondered if it were possible to drown a man with feet like these, since they had all the characteristics of a duck's foot.

There were yet two hours left before it was time to start work for the day, so I hastened to my room and was soon asleep. After breakfast it was a sickly-looking crew that came on deck, some of them very much ashamed, others complaining about not having ice on board, as the fresh water was too warm and did not have the soothing effect it otherwise would have.

The ten Solomon Islanders ate their beans and hardtack as if nothing had happened, much to the disgust of the sailors, who seemed to feel the nauseating effect of this act. The work of moving the lumber was going slowly. It seemed that the sailors could not get enough oatmeal water. Nothing pleased them, everything was wrong. The lumber was too long. It was too heavy. It was not sawed right at the mill. Why did they have to work, and so on and so on?

I realized that if this kept up it would be many weeks before we would be ready to sail for home. With this thought in mind, I jumped into the small boat and pulled ashore to get three quarts of Black and White Scotch whiskey. I felt that after they had had a drink of this famous brand the lumber would move with a will. After giving each one a drink of this murky liquor the lumber seemed to move as if by magic. No longer was it too large and heavy. Each one was trying to outdo the other. The Solomon Islanders were in great danger from the flying two-by-fours, and even the cook was wielding the axe with greater skill as he drove it into the fibrous yams. This was a new departure in the handling of sailors, but so far it was working well. If it was necessary for Scotch whiskey to enter into the discharging of this cargo, I was going to see that each man had enough to stimulate him to even greater results.

While ashore in the afternoon ordering fresh meat and vegetables, I met Captain Kane, who insisted that I pay a visit to His Majesty's ship "Pongon." In walking down the wharf, the Captain noticed a ship in the offing. He seemed interested as he hurried along to the cutter.

"You know," said he, "my eyes are not as good as they should be, and I'll be damned if I know whether she is a coolie or a missionary ship."

Contract labor is used here in working the rice fields and sugar plantations. The coolies sign a five-year contract for sixpence (twelve cents) per day, and all the rice they can eat. They live by themselves and don't associate with the natives, as they consider them unclean because they eat pig. They are very devout in their worship of Allah and adhere strictly to fish and vegetables as a food. They are the type seen in Bombay and Calcutta. Many of them, after being here for a few years, form a company and buy a small sloop of five to ten tons to haul cobra from the different islands to Suva, the capital of the Fijis. The latter town is a distributing center for the Archipelago, and here is where ships of many nations come and load this dried cocoanut for the foreign markets of the world. It is one of the chief industries of these islands.

On boarding the revenue cutter, I noticed the native crew standing around the gangway. They all came to a salute, as their proud Captain swung over the rail. Their uniform resembled that of the policemen, but instead of a red border in a blue field, it was white. This white border with the white-washed hair gave them a clean and wholesome look, very different from the policemen.

Captain Kane led the way to the bridge, and, picking up a pair of binoculars, he made out the strange craft to be a missionary ship. "You will notice," said he as he handed the glasses to me, "that she has painted ports,— damn them painted ports, I know what it means, not a blasted drink as long as she is here. And that's not all, when them missionaries come ashore, especially the older women, all a person sees around here is Hell's burning fires."

The coming of the missionary ship held no charm for Captain Kane. His proud and dignified bearing gave way to that of a child, or one who has lost a near and dear friend. "It is too damned bad," he shouted, "that she should come here at this time; I and a few old friends were about to have a little party." Here he pulled his cheese-cutter cap down with a jerk, so that the bleary eyes were no longer visible.

"And now I suppose I'll have to be converted again. Yes, Hell and damnation, I have been converted to every religion that was ever heard of. Oh, yes, they commercialize it down here, and we all chip in to keep the brass work shining on the missionary ships."

Here Captain Kane made a hasty exit from the good ship "Pongon" and laid out a course for the Pier Hotel, saying: "Little does the world know the troubles that some people have who are trying to do their duty to their God and their King."

At half-past four in the afternoon the missionary ship dropped anchor about a cable's length off our starboard bow. Her crew were dressed in man-o'-war uniforms. They lowered a boat, and as they pulled ashore I could see five portly-looking dames sitting in the stern. They were discussing our ship, and, from the scowling glances they gave us, I felt that we were safe in standing by to repel boarders. They cast loving glances at His Majesty's ship "Pongon," perhaps consulting as to what form of baptism would be most impressive for Captain Kane.

The crew had no desire to go ashore this evening. The last strenuous night and a hard day's work, had left them in a rather sullen mood. Even Old Charlie and Riley were not on speaking terms. Swanson's jaw showed the mark of a belaying-pin, and he seemed quite conscious of it as he chewed his evening meal. The web-toed Russian-Finn looked as if the hum of the mosquito would be a welcome lullaby to the land of dreams.

The cook, though silent and morose, would lift his head occasionally from the dishes to listen to the natives singing their evening hymn, "Shall We Gather at the River Where Bright Angels' Feet Do Tread." Anything with angels in it was displeasing to our cook. He even seemed to take a sudden dislike to Toby as he kicked him out of the galley door, exclaiming, "Get out of here, damn you; I suppose they will be putting wings on you before long."

The Solomon Islands workmen, although tired from the day's work, were laughing and chatting in their native tongue as they circled around a large dishpan of Mulligan stew.

Knives and forks were not much in evidence, the natives preferring to use their hands to eat with. Although trained for centuries to eat in this manner, I must say that the cook's Mulligan stew kept them guessing. I decided that tomorrow, if perchance the cook should arise under the refining influence of a good night's rest, I would ask him to thicken the Mulligan stew in the interest of the Solomon Islanders.

The discharging of cargo was progressing satisfactorily, since we now had the deck load off, and were commencing on the hold. In a few days I had hopes of clearing from Suva and starting on our long voyage home.

CHAPTER XXIII

FIJI ROYALTY — LOCAL COLOR — VISITORS TO THE SHIP

Today I met the royal family of the Fiji Islands. The King, although old, was a very impressive figure, with his long white kinky hair and massive bushy eyebrows. His color was that of a mulatto, a higher type than that of the native Fijians. He wore a loose white tunic cut off at the elbows, and girdled around him was what looked like a homespun sheet. This garment was twisted and tucked tight around the hips, the lower folds falling loosely above the knee; the legs were muscular and strong, and the calves bulged out as if inflated with air. The feet were ugly, long and broad, and the toes resembled those of a starfish. No matter what the angle from which one viewed them, there would always be a toe pointing towards one.

The two princesses were gaily attired in blue

checked Mother Hubbards. This long and flowing garment made them look like our North American squaws. In features they resembled the Samoan type of women.

The Prince, of stately bearing, wore a costume similar to that of his royal father, but his most distinguishing characteristic was the number twelve boots he wore. He seemed particularly interested in those massive hides, as he told me how he came to be their proud possessor. There was no last large enough on the island, and again there was a shortage of leather, so it came to pass that some local astronomer measured the altitude of his Highness' feet, and this measure, sealed in a conch shell, was cast adrift and floated away to an Australian port, where it finally drifted into the hands of one of Dickens' migrating cobblers, who filled the order and waxed them together.

While discussing with the King the starry banner as it floated from the mast head of the "Wampa," my attention was attracted to the silent and lonesome figure of a man, descending the hill beyond the town. As this melancholy figure wended its way among the palms, I could make out the pea jacket and cheese-cutter cap of Captain Kane. As he approached he wore a troubled and anxious look as if in fear, but when he recognized the royal family, his expression gave way to a more pleasing one. He spat out a large chew of tobacco, and slapping the King on the shoulder, "How in Hell did you know the missionary ship was in?"

"Oh," replied the King, "we see flag on hill."

Captain Kane explained to me that when a missionary ship puts in to Suva they raise a flag on one of the largest hills back of the town. That signals to the natives for miles around that there are big doings in Suva. Captain Kane and the royal family evidently did not have much in common, for he grabbed me by the arm and led the way to the Pier Hotel, leaving the royal family gazing and wondering if they could not have made a better bargain with the Stars and Stripes than with the Union Jack of old England.

At the Pier Hotel, Mrs. Fagan greeted us with a smile. As she passed the Old Tom to Captain Kane she remarked, "Sure'n me eyes haven't rested upon you for days, Captain Kane. 'Tis sick I thought you were." Here she gave me a roguish wink.

Before replying, Captain Kane filled his bumper, leaving very little room for the soda, and took a step toward the door to see if the coast were clear. Satisfied that everything was in his favor, he reached for the glass of Old Tom, and with one gulp and a gurgling sound as if running over pebbles, the Old Tom disappeared to its last resting place. He pulled out a much worn bandana handkerchief, and wiping his mouth and beard he said to Mrs. Fagan, "No, I have not been sick, I have been a very busy man of late. But if this incessant singing and praying keeps up I am pretty damned sure I will get sick." Mrs. Fagan interrupted, saying: "Captain, how long are the missionaries going to remain?" "They will stay here until they have every one of us converted again," moaned the Captain.

Mrs. Fagan adjusted a large tortoise-shell comb in her hair, and straightening out her hand-embroidered flounces in her white dress, remarked, "Shur'n it's poor business we do be having when the missionary ship comes in."

"Mrs. Fagan," said I, "give us another drink. And won't you join us?"

"Ah, and it's seldom I ever touch it, but I will

take a little drop of Burke's Irish just to be sociable with you."

After Captain Kane had three bumpers of Old Tom the world had a different aspect for him; even the old gray-haired missionaries weren't so bad after all. They had to make a living like the rest of us. But at times they were objectionable, especially when the gin was awash in the bilges.

On the way down to the wharf Captain Kane promised to take me for a drive in the country, as he felt it would be a great relief to be away at least one day from the missionaries. While pulling off to the "Wampa," I was amused, as a canoe glided past me, to see a native make use of his breech-cloth for a sail. He unwound about two yards of cloth from around his waist and fastened it to two bamboo poles that were about three feet apart. After tying this calico wrapping at the top and bottom of the poles he had a square sail. The square sail with a fair wind made it easy for the native; he leaned back on his steering oar, evidently well pleased with such favorable conditions.

When I came alongside, I noticed that the crew looked me over very critically, as if wondering why I stayed away so long. As it was now one hour past grog time they wore anxious looks. A growl here and a grunt there were all that greeted me. But after each getting a jolt of Scotch, their expressions changed to a smacking of lips, and a heave-aho on the six-by-sixes.

After supper the missionary boat came alongside, and two elderly women came aboard and asked if there were any Christians among the crew. I informed these sanctified-looking ladies that I had my " doots," but would be pleased to escort them to the crew's quarters where they could make their own diagnosis. I left them to go down the scuttle hatch leading to the forecastle and beat a hasty retreat to the cabin, fearing that I might have to share some of Captain Kane's misery.

While entering in the log book the events and progress of the day, I realized from the sounds coming from the fore part of the ship, that the old ladies were making some headway with the crew. As the sound took volume, I could hear them singing, " Pull for the shore, sailors, pull for the shore, heed not the tempest's roar but bend to the oar."

The cook, putting away his clean dishes, said, "What in Hell has got into those fellows this evening?"

I told him that they were having a very sociable visit from the ladies who ran the missionary ship, and that no doubt they would be pleased to pay him a friendly visit. The cook threw the dishes to the pantry shelf, and slamming the pantry door exclaimed, "Keep them away from me; I'm in no mood to discuss religious philosophy to-night."

After giving each member of the crew a small Bible, and praying for our souls in the safe passage home, the old missionary women shoved off for the shore, apparently not at all pleased with their evening's work.

If they had brought about four quarts of Scotch whiskey on board they would have had no trouble in converting the crew, for even the cook could be reconciled to any form of religion, old or new, as long as the Scotch flowed freely.

CHAPTER XXIV

A Drive With Captain Kane — Razorback Rampant

The next day Captain Kane and I started for our drive into the island with an old battered two-seated rig. The horse, though old in years, had a look of being well taken care of, and was rather inclined to shy as he gazed at an unfamiliar palm or cocoanut tree. I hesitatingly offered to spell the Captain off, and asked him to let me drive awhile. He turned on me very angrily and said, " There is no damned ship that ever sailed the seas that required more careful steering than this horse does. One has got to know just how much helm to give him. If you should put it hard over and get him on the home tack all Hell couldn't stop him until he reached the stable. Oh, I know him," continued the Captain, " he has a mouth on him that will hold like the devil's claw on a windlass."

As we drove through the rice fields, I noticed that Hindoos were doing the work; here and there could be seen the lazy natives asleep under the trees. "My object," said the Captain, as he coaxed the old horse past a flying turban that seemed to be coming unfastened from its wearer, "my object in taking you on this trip is to show you the result of a hurricane that happened here twelve years ago. It will not be necessary for me to discuss the velocity of the hurricane, you'll be able to judge for yourself when we pass that village ahead. But," continued the Captain, "for God's sake don't talk above a whisper while I steer Timbuctoo" (for this was the horse's name) "through the palm village. You can see by the action of his head that he is about to make heavy weather of it."

I must say that the old horse had taken a new lease of life; he did not seem to be conscious of his cocked ankles or the spavins or other conspicuous growths that covered his legs. With head erect, arched neck and ears pitched forward, he was not at all particular about using his front feet, but rather inclined to do the cake walk, and always waiting a chance to turn and bolt for home. This was worrying the Captain, for he said anxiously, "I have driven him many times, but never have I seen him act like this. It's these hellish Fijian huts with their palm-covered roofs that are getting on his nerves."

Things were going along about as well as could be expected until we were about at the center of the straggling village. Then it happened that from out a palm-covered hut strolled a razor-back hog, seemingly unconcerned as to our presence and not inclined to observe the rules of the road. The Captain smelled danger, as he warped an extra turn of the lines around his hands, and remarked rather nervously, "There's going to be Hell here in about a minute."

Timbuctoo felt as uncomfortable as his driver; he too sensed the danger of this razor-backed hog. Captain Kane relaxed his hold on the reins to adjust his cheese-cutter cap to a more seaworthy position. While doing so the hog stopped in front of Timbuctoo. All would even then have been well had it not been for the curiosity of this hungry-looking razor-back. I suggested to the Captain that I get out and drive the hog away. "Hell and damnation, no," roared the

Captain,' "keep your seat, I will pass under his quarter."

Timbuctoo veered to starboard under the steady hand of Captain Kane. This move was in accordance with the rules of the road, but unfortunately it proved fatal, for it exposed Timbuctoo's warty legs to the hungry hog. He evidently thought that this was a new kind of crop that did not require rooting, which, to judge from the two large rings in his nose, was a lost art with him.

Before the Captain could brace his clubby boots against the dash-board the razor-backed hog reached out with his long mouth and took hold of Timbuctoo's most conspicuous wart, which was dangling on the right hind leg. When Timbuctoo felt this smarting insult he decided not to await orders from his venerable driver. Grasping the bit in his mouth, he started full speed ahead. "There he goes," roared the Captain, "and God knows when he will stop."

Dan Patch had nothing on Timbuctoo. The cocoanut trees looked like telephone poles as one sees them while riding on the Twentieth Century Limited. "I would not care a damn how far he would run," sang out the Captain as if shouting to a man on the topsail yard in a gale of wind, " if I had not promised to make a speech at the missionary meeting to-night."

" Let me try him, Captain? " said I.

" You try him," said he, " what in Hell do you know about animals? There is no living man could do anything with him now, he has too much damn steam up, all we can do is to trust to luck and keep our helm in midship and let him run before it."

After running about two miles he seemed to realize that the Captain was still with him and not, as he expected, back with the razor-backed hog. Very much disappointed, he broke into a dog trot, much to the relief and satisfaction of the Captain. As he withdrew his number tens, which had perforated through the dashboard, he said, " Well, I have never come through a storm and lost as little canvas as on this here passage."

Timbuctoo had no desire to set the fisherman's staysails, he was content to slow down to a walk.

" Now," said the Captain, " let me get my bearings. Before we met the razor-back, I was going to show you the results of a hurricane as we know them in the Fijis."

After Captain Kane had read the various logarithms in regard to his position, he decided that with the hypothenuse over the base the sine lay ahead and after driving about one-half mile, we came to a large boulder alongside the narrow road. "How much does that boulder weigh?" sniffed the Captain.

"Oh," said I, "about four tons."

"Would you believe," said he, "that during the hurricane of twelve years ago this boulder was carried a distance of three miles?" The Captain was somewhat injured at my not showing more enthusiasm. I must say that the boulder story was hard to absorb, although from its present position on the surface of the ground it showed that it had been moved there recently by some force other than the hand of man.

Taking a chew of tobacco and damning Timbuctoo for daring to rub his foaming mouth on his pea jacket, he said, "You may not believe that this was moved by the hurricane. By God, I can prove it and prove it I will when we reach

Suva." Evidently he hoped to invoke the testimony of some of the worthies who drink their Scotch to the lullaby of the sad sea waves. On our way back to Suva I was impressed by the scenery of the interior of the island, the rolling hills, the native timber resembling California redwood in color, the tall cocoanut trees, the frequent smell of the pineapple, an occasional glimpse of a date palm trying to rear its head from amongst the tropical foliage, claiming a riparian right to the native shrubbery.

Timbuctoo, on the way back to Suva, was slipping it off as well as he could after his recent flight. The razor-back hog recalled early memories to me of the country I knew when I was a boy. The rings in their noses were no new things to me in that far-off country. The coming of the new potato crop held much charm for the Irish hog, but unfortunately the English landlord claimed a prior right in lieu of rent, and poor Barney was subjected to the cruel and unmerciful treatment of having horseshoe nails twisted in his nose.

The Captain was in a rather sullen mood as we drove back. Having had nothing to drink

but the milk from the cocoanut, he exclaimed:
"Why in Hell don't some one start a half-way house out here for the benefit of those who admire and travel these islands?"

CHAPTER XXV

Homeward Bound — The Stowaway

Having cleared the English customs and with a clean bill of health, we were ready to sail. The pilot was on board and his boat's crew had a line fast through the stern chalk so that we could tow them with us clear of the channel reef. Once clear of the reef all that remained to do was to haul the pilot boat alongside and have this servant of His Majesty climb down the Jacob's ladder and into the boat which would bear him away to the spot where the sound of the surf merged into the music of the clinking glass.

While giving orders to rig out slip lines for him I heard a familiar voice on the wharf sing out "Bon voyage, bon voyage." I looked up to see the portly figure of Captain Kane. He looked as if he had slept in his clothes. His pea jacket had many wrinkles in the back and in front it was inclined to roll up toward his chin.

I jumped ashore to say good-bye to this kind, if groggy old sea dog, shook him by the hand, and thanked him for my trip to the interior of the island, saying that I hoped to see him again.

"You know," he said, "I am getting old, but the smell of the Stockholm tar, the white flowing sails, the squeaking blocks, the clink of the capstan, bring back memories of long ago, and, damn it all, it makes me young again."

Captain Kane laid great stress on the hurricane season, as January, February and March were the months to be dreaded in the South Seas. After seeing the boulder that had been hurled by the last hurricane on these islands, I was hoping that I should be well enough to the northward, so that if one should come I would be out of the storm center, and therefore out of danger. The pilot was nervously pacing up and down the main deck anxious to get me away from the wharf and out to sea. Possibly a game of chess had been left unfinished. I jumped aboard and ordered the foresail and main jib set. With this done and the slip lines hauled aboard, the "Wampa" glided away from the wharf as if propelled by steam.

With the aftersails spread and set to the southeast trades, and sheets trimmed to the wind, we were not long in clearing the channel reef and getting out into open water. After the pilot left I ordered the topsails set. The breeze was fair, and I was anxious to clear Bangor Island and get to the westward of it before darkness set in.

The crew looked happy even after their night's debauch, some were whistling, others humming familiar ditties. Riley could be heard singing "Rolling Home Across the Sea" from his position on the foretopmast, as he changed the topsail to windward, a job which is usually done with very little sentiment of home or any other place.

Distance was shutting out the tall green palms around Suva, and the town itself was just a speck on the horizon. Taking careful cross-bearings of Bangor Island, so as to avoid the dangers and submerged coral reefs that project from it, I ordered the staysails set to increase our speed so that with darkness I would be well to the westward.

Our staysails were put away and stowed in the fore peak when we came into port. The second mate went forward to get them up, and Swanson went down to bend a line around them before hauling them on deck. He had been down in the fore peak only a minute before he came up the ladder running very excitedly and saying that there was a dead man lying on the staysails. The crew, much upset by this remark, slunk away from the fore peak hatch as if deadly fumes were coming from within, so I got a lantern and went down to see the supposed dead man. I was confronted by a Hindoo stowaway.

He was so weak from the heat of the fore peak and thirst that he seemed to have little life left in him. I called up to the deck above for a couple of men to come down and give me a hand to carry him. Old Charlie and Riley cautiously felt their way down, Riley giving orders to the crew above not to stand too close to the small hatch, as it might be necessary for him to ascend with all possible speed and he did not care to have any obstruction to his flight. Old Charlie approached with his usual forebodings. The finding of the dead Hindoo, in his estimation, meant nothing less than doom and destruction to all on board.

Riley was more cheerful when he found that there was little chance of physical danger from the supposed dead man. Bending the rope around him and carrying him to the mouth of the hatch, I shouted to the crew on deck to haul away very gently. We steered him up the hatch and landed him on deck without any serious bumps. The cool breeze restored him, and when we forced some water down his throat he began to show signs of life.

I went aft to get a glass of Scotch whiskey, knowing that this would stimulate the heart action. After taking a teaspoonful, his moaning changed to some kind of Hindoo gibberish. This change seemed to amuse the crew. They no longer looked gloomy and down in the mouth, but seemed very willing to help him in his fight for life. As he lay there I was seized with a very inhuman and selfish impulse. The night shades of the tropical evening were becoming conspicuous in the western horizon, the run on the log showed the "Wampa" sixteen miles to the southward and westward of Suva harbor, with the southeast point of Bangor Island bearing two points on the starboard bow.

Should the Hindoo stowaway come back to life, it would be necessary to tack ship and put back to Suva in order to put him ashore.

U. S. alien laws are well known to sea-faring men. This stowaway had no money, no position, and all that he had in the way of clothes was a thin pair of pants. Should unfavorable conditions prevent my putting him ashore, I would be forced to carry him to San Francisco. Once there I knew what the immigration authorities would do to me or to the owners. More than likely I should have to pay his passage back by steamboat to the Fiji Islands. With darkness approaching it was not my intention to put back to Suva and run the risk of striking the reef at the entrance of the harbor. For these reasons, I should much prefer a sea burial for the Hindoo stowaway.

While these hard and unsympathetic thoughts were passing before the visible horizon of my mind, I was nevertheless attracted by his delicate and artistic form. The long and straight black hair, the finely molded ears, the aquiline nose, the perfect profile, the well-rounded chin, the sensual mouth with its uniform white teeth were truly oriental of high caste. An unusual type for a Fijian contract laborer.

I was deeply impressed with his boyish figure as he lay struggling for breath on the deck. Suddenly I was seized with an impulse of sympathy for this frail-looking creature. Grasping the bottle of Scotch I pressed it to his lips and poured some down his throat. This act caused him to strangle. After fighting for breath he opened his eyes and sat up against the hatch combings.

His eyes were bright and fiery and seemed to penetrate through one like an X-ray. They took in the situation at a glance. He realized that he was out at sea. His gaze alternated from the flowing sail to the members of the crew. His eye finally rested on Swanson, he being the most brutish looking sailor of those who were standing around, and therefore the most to be feared. I spoke to the Hindoo and said, "How long have you been on board?"

"Oh," said he, "I have been down there," pointing to the fore peak, "for three days." He spoke English without an accent. Then he told how he had swam off to the ship, while we were still lying at anchor, and said that he had no idea that we would have been delayed so long before putting to sea.

I then told him that it would be impossible to carry him to the United States of America. Although weak from heat and hunger, he staggered to his feet and kissed my hand, crying, " Oh, please, Captain, take me along with you. I cannot live there under these horrible conditions, working for sixpence a day with nothing to eat but curry and rice. I will work for you, I will do anything, only take me away from here."

I deeply resented my previous thought of disposing of this intelligent Hindoo. The picture this outcast made standing there trembling, with tears streaming down his boyish face, pleading as though his heart would break, was getting the best of me. Very few men of the sea can stand tears and emotion. Although hardened by years of kicks and knocks, the old-time sailor would much prefer a knock-down and drag-out to any signs of agitation. Many of the crew themselves consciously looked to windward and wiped away a rusty tear.

While the Hindoo was still pleading, Swanson stepped up to me and between sobs said, "I wish you would take him along, sir, I have no one in the world to care for, and I can easily spare the forty dollars that you say will be necessary for him to enter the United States." With this offer coming from a man like Swanson, I was as much overcome as the Hindoo was, in his pleading for liberty to be taken away from the low and dirty castes of Bombay and Calcutta which furnish labor for the Fiji Islands. He thanked Swanson by gracefully bowing and said, turning to me, "I am sure you can make some use of me on your voyage home." This statement proved true, for had it not been for the stowaway, this narrative would never have been written.

The Socialist cook was standing with his back up against the galley, deeply impressed with this new possibility. From the way he ran to make milk toast for the Hindoo, one would think that at last he had discovered a new clay to mold and construct and pattern after his own impressions.

CHAPTER XXVI

THE MYSTERIOUS HINDOO

With the Hindoo question solved and the fisherman's staysails set, Suva was lost in the distance and remained but a memory. By the time the studded diamonds in their azure setting were twinkling in all the splendor of a Southern sky, we were well to the westward of Bangor Island. We had nothing to fear from coral reefs until we neared the Gilbert group, which lay east of the 180th meridian and north and south of the Equator.

After the Hindoo had eaten the milk toast and found that he was in the midst of friends, sailing away to a country where opportunity knocks on the door of hovels, he no longer looked the slave to his master. He refused to bunk in the forecastle, preferring to sleep under the forecastle head. The tropical nights were warm, and for the time being this was a comfortable part of the ship in which to sleep. The crew were kind enough to furnish blankets for him, in fact, were willing to give him anything they had, for they considered him an unusual guest.

At ten o'clock I turned in and left orders with the second mate to call me at midnight. By that time I knew that if we held our present rate of eleven knots per hour, we should be far enough to the westward to change the course, and haul her more northerly. Coming on deck at eight bells and getting the distance run on the log, I went back to my room to measure the distance on the chart before changing the course. I decided to run one more hour before changing to the northward.

Old Charlie was at the wheel, and it seemed from the way he was clearing his throat that he was anxious for a chat. But discipline forbade. I walked forward to look at the sails, and see if they needed sweating up. While looking around I ran into Riley, who as usual was smoking his clay pipe, with its black bowl and short stem. It was strong enough of nicotine to drive a wharf-rat to suicide.

"Riley," said I, "no doubt you are happy that we are on the last leg of our voyage."

Before answering he gave a few heavy puffs on the old dudeen to insure its not going out. While he was doing this I immediately changed for a new position to windward, for to be caught to leeward of these deadly fumes was to share the fate of the wharf-rat.

"Well," said Riley, "I am, and I am not."

"Come," I replied, "what is it that troubles you?" Thinking that I had found the source of his discontent, I added,— "Surely, you can't expect me to feed you on Scotch whiskey all the passage home? What little there is on board must be kept for medicine. Just think what might have happened to the poor Hindoo had I not had a little Scotch left on board."

At the mention of the Hindoo's name Riley stepped up close to me, saying, "Whisht, and it is that what is troubling me, it is that damned coolie," and he pointed to the forecastle.

"Surely," I protested, "you are not afraid of that poor weak creature."

Riley fastened down the tin cover to his pipe so as to secure the remains of the tobacco for future use. Economy of tobacco is strictly observed on long voyages. Even the ashes have an intrinsic value among sailors, like the kindling wood of a coal stove. Tucking the pipe away in the folds of his breeches, he said:

"Ho, ho, and it is afraid you would have me! Shure'n I am afraid of nothing in the say, and I will be damned if I will be afraid of anything on top of it."

"Well, what about the Hindoo, what harm can he do to you?"

"Oh, it's the divil a bit he will be doing me. It's his snaky movements and his ferret eyes that is getting on me nerves. During the dog-watch," continued Riley, "we fixed a place under the foc's'le head for the coolie, giving him what blankets we could spare. At eight o'clock our watch below turned in. Says I to Dago Joe, 'Turn down the glim.' 'I will blow it out,' says he. 'Not by a damn sight,' says I. 'Shur'n we are liable to scrape our bottom on an auld coral reef around here, and it isn't Mike Riley that is going to get caught like a rat in a trap.' The Dago is a reasonable man to talk to, and with that he turns the light very low. About eleven o'clock I woke up along the hearing Broken-Nosed Pete snoring. After throwing me auld shoe at him, I rolled over with me face to the scuttle hatch, to get meself another nap before eight bells, when I see the Hindoo standing there at the bottom of the ladder. I rubbed me eye to make sure it wasn't desayving me. Pulling meself together, I says to meself, says I, 'Whativer he is, he is there for no good purpose.' Begob, the strangest thing about the coolie was that he did not move a muscle, but stood there like a statue, staring straight into me eye.

"I shouted to the Dago to turn up the light, which is within easy reach of him. Says I, 'Things are not as they should be down here.' With me eye still on the Hindoo, Dago Joe turned up the light. I declare to me Maker when the light was turned up the Hindoo had disappeared.

"'That's damned strange,' says I to Dago Joe. 'Be Hivens he was standing there not a minute ago,' and when I comes up on deck at eight bells I looked under the foc's'le head and there he is, fast asleep. So I lights me poipe, and takes a look over the sea to leeward of the foresail, to see if we are still in sight of land. While I am standing there humming a bit av an auld ditty, all of a sudden I felt meself in the presence of something uncanny, and turning around quick-like, there stood the coolie. Ses I to him, ses I:

"'What are you up to, me boy?'

"'Oh,' says the coolie, 'the wash on the prow is disturbing to my peaceful slumbers. I should much prefer being crooned to sleep by the waving branches of a Himalayan evergreen.'

"Ses I, 'Me coolie friend, no more of your palavering. Back to bed with you, and stay there.' I looked at him again, and, shure, Howly St. Patrick, he disappears like he did in the foc's'le."

"Where is he now Riley?"

"Begobs, and I don't know, sir."

I went forward to see the strange visitor who seemed to be causing Riley so much misery. There, under the forecastle head, the Hindoo lay, wrapped in his blankets, sound asleep.

"Riley," said I, "you drank too much Scotch last night; be careful that you don't get the Jimmies and jump overboard. If you feel yourself slipping just tie a gasket around you. We need you to work ship on the voyage home."

These insults were too much for Riley. He slunk away to the lookout where Broken-Nosed

Pete would lend a willing ear to his story of the Hindoo and his abuse of me.

At one o'clock, feeling sure of the reefs, I changed the course to N. N. W.

The next morning the Hindoo was eating his breakfast off the forehatch and looking much better than he had on the preceding evening. He rose and thanked me kindly for the interest we had taken in him, saying:

"I feel the pleasure of liberty after my prison term, among those terrible people. As for last night, I was quite comfortable. I can easily adapt myself to the new environment. But although I could not quite understand what the one-eyed man meant when he bent over me in the night, exclaiming, 'There he is, and the divil a move out of him,' I feel nevertheless, that I am in the midst of friends, and I shall do my best to entertain their friendship."

These quaint expressions were pleasing to me, and I continued the conversation. He said that he had had no sea experience. That while going from Bombay to the Fiji Islands he was battened down in the hold with the rest of the coolie labor, and only allowed to walk the deck a short time in the evenings. He was anxious to work and help in any way that he could. The second mate put him to work scrubbing paint-work. There is always plenty of this kind of work to be done on every ship. The Hindoo went to work with a will, as if glad to have the opportunity.

For the next four days the southeast trades held fair, until we were well to the northward of the Fiji group. I was hoping to get east of the 180th meridian before crossing the Equator. This would give me a better slant before I struck the northeast trades. Then in latitude about 30° north we would encounter the westerly winds, which would be fair for the Pacific coast.

I was well pleased with the progress we had made since we left Suva, and I anticipated making a sailing record from the Fijis to San Francisco.

Events had favored us since our departure. The crew were willing and the good ship herself seemed to feel that she was homeward bound. But our outward peace was somewhat broken by the sudden and mysterious illness of the Hindoo, who, after the second day out from Suva refused to eat, complaining of a headache, and later remaining for hours in what appeared to be almost a state of coma.

I was worried by this new disease, and hoped that it would not prove to be contagious. As a precautionary measure, I removed the Hindoo aft to the deceased Captain's cabin. For two days it was with a great effort that he was even aroused to drink a cup of bouillon.

CHAPTER XXVII

The Hurricane

At two o'clock in the morning of our fifth day from Suva, I was awakened by hearing the booms and gaffs swinging as if in a calm. I thought this very strange, as the southeast trades should have held until we were well across the Equator. Rushing up on deck, I was indeed surprised to find the sails hanging in midships, and not a breath from any quarter of the compass.

I ordered the staysails down and the topsails clewed up and made fast, also the flying-jib and outer jib. (These lighter sails in a calm usually flop to pieces, especially where there is a rolling swell.) Away to the eastward I noticed a heavy bank of clouds, but considered this of minor importance, as we were nearing the Equator. It usually means heavy rain, but seldom wind.

Yet this morning there was something out of the ordinary, because of the long swell coming from the northeast, and the sickly and suffocating atmosphere. The unusual stillness was intensified by the murmuring and talking of the crew. The men who were making fast the headsails on the flying jibboom could be heard plainly from the poop deck, growling and swearing as they passed the gaskets around the sails. Such was the funereal quietness of the morning that even the stars were hidden in halos of a yellowish color.

Giving instructions to haul in the log line, I went below to look at the barometer. I was surprised to find it falling. I next consulted a Pacific directory, and found that these unusual conditions preceded a hurricane. This information upset me greatly. I had never experienced a hurricane, but well knew that their force and destructive power was very great.

Before going on deck again, I looked in on the Hindoo in the Captain's room. As usual, he was in a stupor, and looked as if he had not moved since being fed the preceding evening. I did notice from the heaving of the skeleton-like breast, that the breathing was regular, and not intermittent as it had been on the preceding evening.

On deck, I had all the reef-earrings brought up from the lazarette, and got everything in readiness for any emergency.

I was well to the westward of the Gilbert group, but still to the eastward of the 180th Meridian. Should the hurricane come out of the east, I could heave to and ride it out without any danger of fetching up on one of the Gilbert Islands.

In the cabin the barometer was falling so fast that it now showed hurricane weather. I knew that it was only a question of a few hours before we should feel its fury. My experience was limited in the laws of storms. If we were in the storm center it would be necessary to put her into the port tack. By doing this I should be forced south, and back onto the northern isles of the Fiji group, while on a starboard tack I should be driven onto a lee shore of the Gilbert Islands. Either course meant destruction.

With daylight and hot coffee this gloomy situation assumed a more cheerful aspect. While the old sailor has the light of day to guide him over storm-tossed decks, he becomes more tolerant of ship and crew.

At half-past five the white caps could be seen coming from the northeast, and before we got the spanker down the gale struck us, about six points on the starboard bow. The old ship reeled to leeward, with the lee rail under water. The decks were almost perpendicular. It seemed that no power on earth could right her to an even keel again. There were two men at the wheel, trying to keep her off before the gale, but it was of no avail, for she refused to answer her helm, and lay throbbing as if undecided whether to seek a watery grave, or to continue her fight for victory.

Swanson, by a heroic effort, cut the fore and main sheet, and then let go by the run. The tense situation was relieved as the booms flew seaward over the lee rail. We then kept her off before the gale with the wind on the starboard quarter, immediately setting to work to reef the fore and main sail.

By nine o'clock, three hours and a half later, it was no longer a gale, but a hurricane. With three reefs in the foresail and a goose-wing spanker, we ran before it. It was too late to heave to. With such a tremendous sea running it would mean destruction to ship and crew to try the latter move. As it was, the ship was awash fore and aft from seas breaking over her. Should the hurricane hold out for ten or twelve hours more with our present rate of speed we should be dashed to pieces against one of the Gilbert group.

At four bells the velocity of the hurricane was so great that one was in danger of being blown off the schooner. We rigged life-lines on the fore and main decks, also on the poop deck, and by their help the crew managed to keep from being washed or blown overboard. The sea looked like an immense waterfall, one enormous roaring mass of foam. Occasionally from out of this terrible cataract a Himalayan sea would gain in momentum and dash itself against our starboard quarter, submerging the vessel. At such times all that would be identifiable of the "Wampa" would be her rocking spiral masts.

Like a struggling giant she would raise her noble head and shake herself clear of this octopus, shivering, but never spent.

About noon the hurricane jumped suddenly from the northeast to east southeast, without losing any of its velocity. In order to keep running before it, and keep the wind on our starboard quarter we hauled more to the northward and westward, although to do this it was necessary to drive into a beam sea, which made it all the more dangerous. Also the sea was driving from the east southeast and this formed a cross sea.

When these two seas came together, the "Wampa" would rise and poise on them as if on a pivot. In this position, and with the gale blowing on the starboard quarter, her head would be thrown into the beam sea. It looked as if we could not survive. There was constant danger of our being broken up into small pieces. We dropped the peak of the spanker that formed the goose-wing sail, put it into gaskets, and ran with a three-reefed foresail.

We then put the oil-bags over the stern in the hope of quieting these angry seas. But this was useless. While we were fastening the lines that held the oil-bags in the water, a crushing comber came whistling along and filled our stanch little ship again from stem to stern. When she shook herself clear of the boiling foam I noticed that our oil-bags were gone, and with them the Captain's boat which hung from davits over the stern.

Old Charlie and Dago Joe were steering. Old Charlie had a faraway look in his watery eyes as he spoke and said:

"I am afraid, sir, this will be my last trick at this wheel."

I spoke harshly to this old sailor, saying, "To Hell with sentiment, this is no place for it. Watch your steering and don't feel sorry for yourself." Had I known what was so soon to happen I should not have so upbraided this poor harmless old soul. I have often regretted it.

Riley, who was taking no chances, was seemingly not all handicapped by his one eye. Always alert and as agile as a tiger, he went about the decks as if nothing were out of the ordinary, although to hear him talking to himself one would think that he expected to be extinguished by every sea that came. He had about twenty feet of manila rope tied about his waist with the end held in his hand. When a sea would hit us Riley would see it coming, and would pass the rope end around a belaying-pin or anything that he thought would hold his weight.

It was while she cleared herself from the sea that carried away the Captain's boat that I found Riley twisted around the spanker sheet like an eel. It took him some time to extricate himself, always watching the progress of the stern sea, and not seeming to notice his number ten brogans, which had woven themselves into the spanker-sheet falls. The hurricane was raising havoc with Riley's mustache. Having blown all over his face, it looked as if the only way to quiet it would be to put it into a plaster of Paris cast. He finally pulled himself clear of the sheet, exclaiming:

" Be Hivins, and wasn't that a close call —"

Just then Swanson came running aft and reported that the martingale guy had carried away on the flying-jibboom. It was then that my heart sank within me. I knew what to expect. Dismantled,— then to perish at sea!

CHAPTER XXVIII

THE MASTER RETURNS

The thought of our dead captain came to me, of what his will would have been in this crisis of life and death, and I paused to wonder why he had not rested until he was assured that I would not carry his precious treasures back with me. Did he expect this situation, and doubt my ability to cope with it? Action followed thought, and I ordered the second mate and the crew forward to see what could be done with the martingale guy.

Still the humor of the moment appealed to me. As Riley left the poop he shouted, " Be the Holy St. Patrick, it has blown the buttons off me oilskin coat." There was no question about its blowing, but it was also possible that his snakelike position on the spanker-sheet had something to do with the lost buttons.

It was now past noon. None of the crew cared to eat, preferring the wave-swept deck to anything the cook had to offer. The murderer who pays for his crime on the gallows and enjoys his ham and eggs on the morn of execution may be happy indeed, but this does not apply to the sailor. When there is a life and death battle on with the elements, he is there to grab the one last chance if there be one. If not, he prefers a watery grave to claim him with his stomach empty.

The seas kept coming larger, and every time one would break and spend itself on the decks I thought it would be the last, and that she could not arise. But she shook herself clear as she climbed the waves; then again the sea, and again the dread.

I could not leave the poop nor the two men at the wheel. A wrong turn at this howling, raging time, would mean quick despatch to the land of no awakening. Sometimes even the helmsmen grew afraid, but a word of encouragement sufficed to quiet them.

While I was standing to windward of the men at the wheel, watching her every move as she was pitched hither and thither on this crazy spiral sea, she shipped a green sea that shook her from stem to stern. It was with great difficulty that she raised her black hull to the raging storm again. I shouted to the men at the wheel. It was too late. She had broached to with the stern sea on the beam, and the beam sea right ahead.

Then the beam sea submerged her, and by it I was carried across the poop deck, and found myself held under the wheel-box, with both legs pinned in a vise-like grip by the tiller, which extended forward of the rudder-head. Although dazed and strangled by the terrible impact of the water, I managed to twist the upper part of my body towards the wheel and to murmur, " For God's sake keep her off."

My weakened voice was lost in the tempest. There were no ears to hear my pleadings. The men at the wheel were gone. Gone, indeed, to a watery grave, and perhaps the others also. With me it would not take long. Just another raking like the last one, and then the finish. Again the cook's words echoed louder than the raging storm, " Do we finish here? "

As I lay there pinned to the deck, too helpless

to even call aloud, and as it seemed waiting, waiting, for the executioner to spring the deadly trap, I was conscious that the door of the companion-way had closed with a bang so terrific that it sounded above the storm. I twisted my head and shoulders around to see if I dared to hope. There before me stood the Hindoo stowaway. He did not notice me lying there pinned under the wheel-box, nor could I manage to attract his attention.

With opal eyes glowing green and fiery red, he sprang to the wheel, and with magnificent strength pulled on the spokes till they screeched louder than the storm as they were dislodged from their oxidized fittings. Harder and harder he pulled on the wheel. He didn't even notice the seas breaking over him. The mysterious thing about him was that he seemed to know what he was doing. He was keeping her off before it.

In doing this he removed the tiller from my legs. At last I was free. As I struggled and crawled to the weather-rail for support, the Hindoo shouted in clear and ringing tones, in true seamanlike fashion, looking neither to the right nor left, but straight ahead, as if staring into a land-locked harbor. He repeated his order for the second time in a high tenor voice:

"Get an axe out of the donkey-room and cut away the lee martingale guy. Your flying-jibboom is gone overboard and is still held by the lee guy. It is plowing a hole in the port bow."

I knew but one law. The law of self-preservation. My arms were locked tight around the stanchion that supported the weather-rail. That quick command of the Hindoo brought me sharply to the realization that I was not yet given that quick despatch to the land of nowhere, but was still in the flesh, and very much alive. My first rational thought was, "What in Hell is the Hindoo doing at the wheel?" My pride as a sailor resented the affront put upon my ability as a sailor by a stowaway who was daring to assume the command of my ship, and daring to issue orders to me.

Letting go my hold on the stanchion, I cautiously made for the Hindoo helmsman. While in the act, she shipped another drencher. I was carried off my feet and washed away to the lee scuppers. But I managed, by some interposition of Divine Providence, to fasten my arms around the mooring-bitt, thus saving myself from an angry and cruel sea, which seemed to delight in playing with me as a cat does with a mouse, only to swallow me up in its fathomless depths.

Once again she wrenched herself free of the mad swirl and her stern went down until we were in a valley between mountains of water. I realized as I looked up at the bows which seemed to be towering above me, that the flying-jibboom, like a clipped wing, was missing. Like a flash I wondered how the Hindoo knew that the jibboom was gone.

As her stern ascended high into the air, I jumped for the wheel and with an exclamation of joy I shouted, " God in Heaven, the Captain! "

There he stood beside the Hindoo. The dead Captain. The same heavy mustache covered the lower lip. The same fiery eyes that knew no defeat. He was looking straight ahead with muscle-set jaws. He appeared as if in the flesh and ready as of yore to battle with the elements.

Then, like a flash, he vanished, and the Hindoo stood alone, pulling and tugging on the wheel with his supple arms.

He spoke, and his usually high-pitched tenor voice rang out piercingly clear. "Cut away your jibboom, you have no time to lose. Have no fear."

I knew that her former Captain was in command of the ship, and that his masterly seamanship wrought through the Hindoo. I crept forward with new courage to do his bidding.

Huddled together beneath the forecastle-head stood what remained of the crew, who seemed not to know that two of their number were gone. The second mate was praying, and helpless from fear to be of any use in handling the schooner. Riley had his three-inch sailor's rope fast to the windlass with one extra turn around his body. He was taking no chances. Swanson was the only one without fear. When I called for a volunteer to cut away the flying jibboom he made for the axe and rushed onto the sea-swept forecastle-head. As the schooner arose high in the air, he swung over the lee bow and with one stroke of the axe cut away the hemp lanyard that was holding the massive spar from its freedom.

For five hours more we battled with the hurricane. The foretopmast went overboard, and all our boats were smashed into firewood. The lee bulwarks, between the mizzen and mainmast, were washed away, and still the Hindoo held the wheel and issued his orders. Many times I offered to take the wheel, and ordered him to go below. He would wave me away with his hand, saying:

"Not yet,— soon, soon."

About six o'clock, twelve hours and a half after the hurricane struck us, the wind let up some. We then went to work with a will to patch up what was left of the "Wampa," and for the first time since half-past five o'clock that morning, we realized how hungry we were. It was while giving orders to the cook that I looked towards the wheel and saw that the Hindoo was missing.

Calling Swanson to take the wheel as I ran, I rushed to find him. There by the wheel he lay, where he had fallen, limp as a rag,— unconscious. Gathering him easily into my arms, I carried him to the Captain's room, laying him in the bunk as carefully as if he were a babe newborn. For two hours we worked over him, the crew unchidden tiptoeing back and forth in clumsy ministrations, the Socialist cook refusing to leave him. As he finally came back to earth from those astral regions he so easily frequented, a sigh of relief, almost hysterical, went up from the whole ship. Surely there had been enough of tragedy!

Along about eight o'clock the wind fell very light. As there was still a heavy swell running, it would be dangerous to put sail on her for she would shake it into threads.

While walking up and down the poop deck I could hear Riley and the cook working over the stowaway. My thoughts turned to old Charlie and to Dago Joe, who were sleeping their last sleep out there at sea. Had it not been for Him, for Him who had loved his ship, we would all have shared the same merciless fate. What might have happened had I followed my first impulse to cast the Hindoo overboard?

The cook came running up the companion-way very much excited, and said "Come down quick, the Hindoo is showing signs of life." In the Captain's room, under the sickly and only lamp, the frail body was moving from side to side, sometimes making a feeble effort to sit up, often swinging his arms as if to ward off some impending danger. Then he asked for a drink of water and gradually became rational.

When I told him what a wonderful service he had performed, he smiled and said, " Surely you can't mean me." I insisted, telling him in detail how, when two men had been washed overboard, he had seized the wheel and saved the ship. " You must be mistaken," he protested, " I have not been on deck, and I cannot steer, I know nothing whatever about a ship as a sailor. But I have just awakened from a dream that was worse than your Christian Hell."

CHAPTER XXIX

The Home Port

"The wind is from the south-southeast, sir," sang out Swanson from the wheel. Riley gave voice to my impulse when he said, "Thank God, it is the southeast trades again, sir."

The days that followed brought us fine weather and a gentle breeze. We were fortunate enough to escape the doldrums. The southeast trades carried us into the northeast trade winds. In latitude 30° north we struck the westerly winds that blow fair for the Pacific coast of the U. S. A. Fifty-six days from Suva we rounded Lime Point, sailed up Frisco Bay, and dropped the hook off Goat Island.

The owner welcomed me at his office, and was pleased indeed to know that his favorite schooner was once again in her home port.

Later, when we were towed alongside the wharf, the good ship "Wampa" was the object of much speculation among the old hard-shelled water-front men, not so much from her battered condition, although she was minus port bulwarks, foretopmast and flying jibboom, as from some air of mystery which in a conscious way seemed to emanate from the very hull of her. Veterans of the deep who were in port loading new cargoes, would come and go, walking in silence like pall-bearers.

Possibly this was due to the appearance of the Hindoo stowaway, or it may have been that the occult voyage of the "Wampa" had been aired in Rooney's Steam Beer Joint which was at the end of the wharf. Yet with all this hushed solemnity, I do believe that it was I who most sincerely mourned our Captain and the two honest, simple sailormen whose lives had been so unprotestingly given to their duty. Many a voyage have I had since then, but at no time have I ever felt at once so near to Humanity, and to the Infinite. The Hindoo, who had picked up and grown fat on the cook's pea-soup and salt-horse, went to a home which I found for him with a hotel man, who advanced the entry-fee, and put him to work as a porter. He saved his money and, after familiarizing himself with the customs and conventions of the Western people, he moved north to the State of Oregon, where he went into the real estate business, acquiring, up to eight years ago, a goodly sum of money.

The Socialist cook exchanged his greasy dungarees for a pair of hand-me-down creaseless serge pants. With these and a much-worn broadcloth coat that had long withstood gales from the critics of equal distribution, he entered once more the harness of Socialism. With him he took Toby, the black cat, to a life ashore. I believe, though, that his voyage on the "Wampa" had changed his materialistic ideas.

Riley swore that he had made his last trip on windjammers, but that should necessity compel him to take again to the sea, he would sail in a gentleman's yacht. There he would be sure of frequent home ports, each with its black-eyed Susan reigning supreme. But conditions were not as Riley had planned. The steam beer was as plentiful as ever, but the dinero was running low, and he had to take the first thing that offered that would reef and steer. Since then I have met him many times.

Swanson, the most daring and best sailor of the

"Wampa's" crew, went to a navigation school in San Francisco. With his second mate's papers he put off on a long Southern voyage, and after a few years he became captain.

For my services the owner of the "Wampa" promised me the command of a vessel that was overdue from South America, and which was expected any day. After two weeks had passed without news from the South American wanderer, I headed North. The Yukon was calling for men of endurance and men of red blood to come and uncover her hidden treasures.

THE END